"Have you finished with the scientific analysis, Doctor?"

Dan asked her.

"Not yet," Janet retorted. "Any man who expects nothing from females except to have his furniture dusted and his ego pampered doesn't deserve a good woman."

"I expect more." He advanced toward her. "Much, much more."

He was directly in front of her now, standing so close she could feel his body heat.

"You forgot this." He caught her shoulders and pulled her into his arms.

Dear Reader,

Happy Spring! April 1990 is in full bloom—the crocuses are bursting forth, the trees are beginning to bud and though we have an occasional inclement wind, as Shelley wrote in *Ode to the West Wind*, "O Wind, If Winter comes, can Spring be far behind?"

And in this special month of nature's rebirth, we have some wonderful treats in store for you. Silhouette Romance's DIAMOND JUBILEE is in full swing, and this month discover *Harvey's Missing* by Peggy Webb, a delightful romp about a man, a woman and a lovable dog named Harvey (aka George). Then, in May, love is in the air for heroine Lara MacEuan and her handsome, enigmatic hero, Miles Crane, in *Second Time Lucky* by Victoria Glenn.

The DIAMOND JUBILEE—Silhouette Romance's tenth anniversary celebration—is our way of saying thanks to you, our readers. To symbolize the timelessness of love, as well as the modern gift of the tenth anniversary, we're presenting readers with a DIAMOND JUBILEE Silhouette Romance title each month, penned by one of your favorite Silhouette Romance authors. In the coming months, writers such as Marie Ferrarella, Lucy Gordon, Dixie Browning, Phyllis Halldorson—to name just a few—are writing DIAMOND JUBILEE titles especially for you.

And that's not all! Pepper Adams has written a wonderful trilogy—*Cimarron Stories*—set on the plains of Oklahoma. And Laurie Paige has a heartwarming duo coming up— *Homeward Bound*. Be sure to look for them in late spring/ early summer. Much-loved Diana Palmer also has some special treats in store during the months ahead....

I hope you'll enjoy this book and all of the stories to come. Come home to romance—Silhouette Romance—for always!

Sincerely,

Tara Hughes Gavin
Senior Editor

PEGGY WEBB

Harvey's Missing

Published by Silhouette Books New York

America's Publisher of Contemporary Romance

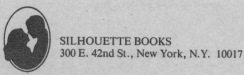

SILHOUETTE BOOKS
300 E. 42nd St., New York, N.Y. 10017

ISBN: 0-373-08712-8

First Silhouette Books printing April 1990

Printed in the U.S.A.

Books by Peggy Webb

Silhouette Romance

When Joanna Smiles #645
A Gift For Tenderness #681
Harvey's Missing #712

PEGGY WEBB

grew up in a large northeastern Mississippi family where the Southern tradition of storytelling was elevated to an art. "In our family there was always a romance or a divorce or a scandal going on," she says, "and always someone willing to tell it. By the time I was thirteen I knew I would be a writer."

Over the years Peggy has raised her two children—and twenty-five dogs. "Any old stray is welcome," she acknowledges. "My house is known as Dog Heaven." Recently her penchant for trying new things led her to take karate lessons. Although she was the oldest person in her class and one of only two women, she now has a blue belt in Tansai Karate. Her karate hobby came to a halt, though, when wrens built a nest in her punching bag. "I decided to take up bird-watching," says Peggy.

A Note From The Author:

Dear Friends,

One of my greatest joys is bringing to life characters you can cherish and letting them tell their stories. Thank you for loving my characters, for enjoying their stories and for telling me how much their romances mean to you.

I wish I could take full credit for Miss Josephine Tobias fighting the dragon with her umbrella in *A Gift for Tenderness* and for Joanna setting up the hero with a broomstick date in *When Joanna Smiles*, but I cannot. My characters won't let me. Just when I think I have control, they go off on a wonderful adventure, and the best I can do is follow along to see what happens.

I thought I finally had control in *Harvey's Missing*. When the lovable mutt Harvey came to me and demanded a story, I created a high-powered master for him, Dan Albany, a criminal lawyer. Alas, Dan refused to be a lawyer. He insisted that he was a soccer coach. Naturally I argued with him. After all, I was the one writing the story. I threatened and cajoled, but he remained staunch. Finally I gave in. I agreed to let him be a soccer coach if he would promise to be a hero I could love.

And he is. I hope you will fall in love with him, too. I hope you will cherish all the heroes and heroines who are bold enough to share their lives and who are generous enough to let their stories be told.

All my best wishes,
Peggy Webb

Chapter One

Harvey was missing. He hadn't come home for the past two weekends, and Janet was getting worried. As she parked her car in front of her condominium, she decided she'd have to do something about him. Soon. But first she had to soak her feet. It had been a long day at the clinic.

A light rain was falling, and when she got out of the car she pulled her coat close against the chill.

"Is that you, Janet?"

Her next-door neighbor, Mr. Jeddidiah Rakestraw—fond of saying he was seventy years spry—always greeted her that way. Because of the cold weather, only his head stuck out his front door.

She smiled at him. "It's me, Mr. Jed. How have you been today?"

"Can't complain, except about the weather. Never thought when I left Chicago and moved down here that I'd see snow pretty near every January, even if it is just a few flakes most times. Snow in Mississippi. Nobody in Chicago believes me.''

"You think it's going to snow?"

"Could be." Mr. Jed inched farther out his door as Janet started up her sidewalk. In his corduroy pants and a sweater with leather elbow patches he reminded her of an aging Faulkner. "How about a cup of hot chocolate?''

"That sounds good. Your place or mine?''

His smile was so big she could see the gap where four teeth were missing. "Yours. Wouldn't do for you to come over here, me being sweet on you and all. One of us might get carried away.''

Chuckling, she crossed the tiny patch of front yard that separated the two condos and took the old man's arm to steady him. Two things she loved about her condo were Mr. Jed and her postage-stamp yard. Mr. Jed had a joyful spirit that gave her a lift after dealing with sick children all day, and her yard was so small that it never accused her of neglect by looking naked without all the petunias, zinnias, forsythia and whatever else ordinary, sane adults in Tupelo planted in their flower beds.

Janet fitted the key into her lock and pushed open her front door. The fragrance of peach potpourri greeted her. She stood a moment, inhaling the sweet scent and enjoying the peace of her house; then she hung her coat on the hall tree and led Mr. Jed through her polished hallway into her living room. It was a small, comfortable room, Wedgwood blue and white with touches of peach, and it was as sparkling fresh and clean as only a one-person room can be. Janet put her hand on the back of a wing chair and stood a moment, just smiling. She loved order and peace and quiet, and only rarely did she get lonely.

"Awful quiet in your house," Mr. Jed remarked as he sat down in a chair beside the fireplace.

"It is. Especially since Harvey's not here. Have you seen him lately?"

"That big stray mutt that comes over here every weekend?"

"Yes. I haven't seen him in a couple of weeks."

"Probably courting. That's what everybody else is doing these days—everybody except you."

Janet waved her hand in airy dismissal. "I'm a career woman, Mr. Jed. You and Harvey are enough for me."

She escaped to her kitchen and prepared the hot chocolate with the same swift efficiency she displayed in her work. What she had told him was true: she *was* satisfied with her career. Not that she didn't like children. On the contrary, she loved them. That's why she had chosen pediatrics. But her job demanded so much physical and emotional energy that she didn't have enough left over for a serious relationship. At least that's what Guy Maxwell had told her three years ago when he'd broken their engagement. He'd probably been right.

She set the hot chocolate on a tray and went out to join Mr. Jed for a relaxing cup and a neighborly chat.

By the time she'd escorted him home, it was dark and the wind and rain had picked up speed. She felt a winter storm in the air and thought of Harvey, out there on the streets somewhere, cold and friendless and hungry.

"Harvey," she called into the darkness. No friendly dog face appeared. No wagging tail thumped her front door, and no big pink tongue licked her hand. She couldn't imagine spending another Friday evening without Harvey.

She ducked inside the condo, bundled into her winter raincoat and went back out to the car. This was no time to soak her feet; she had to find her dog.

Her condo was on the corner of Jefferson and Madison, directly across from the library. She took the Madison Street exit, turned the corner at Jefferson and cruised slowly down the street, looking right and left for the mutt who was part golden retriever, part mournful hound dog, and all heart. At the First Baptist Church she turned north on Church Street toward the elementary school. Harvey liked children. He could be on the playground, waiting for a group of Girl Scouts or watching a late soccer practice. Though why anybody would be practicing in this weather, she couldn't imagine.

The rain came down in earnest as she drove slowly along. She passed a large man wrapped in a heavy raincoat and carrying a big black umbrella. He looked sinister on the dark, lonely street. Not many people walked the streets in weather like this, certainly not in a residential section of town. She started to pass him, then changed her mind. Obviously she was overworked to be thinking of one of her fellow citizens as sinister. Tupelo was the friendliest town she knew, and besides the man might have seen Harvey. Feeling a little bit foolish, she backed up and pressed the button that lowered her window.

"Excuse me," she called.

The man jerked up his head, as if she had startled him. There was nothing sinister about his blue eyes. Or his face. Under the streetlights it looked as open and friendly as a dance club on ladies' night.

"Yes?"

The voice was nice, too, she decided. Rich and crisp, like dark red apples.

"I'm looking for my dog—Harvey. Have you seen a large tan dog?"

The big man ambled slowly toward her car. He didn't walk or stroll; he ambled, as if the sky were pouring sunbeams on his head instead of raindrops—as if he had nothing but time on his hands.

"That's a funny coincidence. I'm looking for a dog myself. George. A big, shaggy mutt with reddish hair and a tail that wags all the time." The man was beside her car now, and he leaned into her window. "I don't suppose you've seen him?"

His smile was sincere and a little crooked. She smiled back.

"No. I'm afraid not. Sorry I can't help you."

"Me, too." He patted the car door almost absently and looked as if he were going to say something else; then he backed away. "Good luck."

"You, too."

As she drove off, she glanced in her rearview mirror. He was still standing there, not quite on the sidewalk but not quite in the street, either, the big umbrella dangling by his side, raindrops pouring over his head. His wet hair made a dark cap of curls around his face. With the streetlights shining down on his head, he looked noble.

She was at the end of the block before she realized she hadn't even glanced in the direction of the school. Harvey could have been standing on his hind legs saluting the flag in the front yard for all the attention she'd been paying.

Mentally chiding herself, she rounded the corner, scanning the thick hedges that bordered the football field. A block down the street she parked her car. The only way she could possibly find her dog in the dark was to make a thorough search of the campus on foot with her flashlight. She decided to start with the football field.

After the woman drove off, it took Dan Albany two minutes to snap out of whatever spell he was in. He'd thought himself acquainted with every good-looking woman in Tupelo, but somehow he'd missed that auburn-haired beauty in the Porsche. Classy car, classy lady, he thought. And she liked dogs. That was a plus. If she also liked cream-filled cupcakes, greasy hamburgers, soggy fries, kids and soccer games in the rain, she'd be just about perfect. But he hadn't even asked her name.

Shaking his head to clear it, he sent raindrops flying. With a sigh, he lifted his umbrella and continued down the street in search of his dog. He even laughed aloud at his foolish fancies.

"Well, Coach," he said in that jocular way he had of addressing himself when he felt he needed a good talking to, "it's just as well. Ladies driving Porsches aren't usually the old-fashioned type who enjoy life on a shoestring budget." Not that he was looking, anyhow. Life had a wonderful way of just happening, and he figured one day his sweet, old-fashioned dream woman would waltz into his life. Though why it hadn't happened in forty years, he couldn't say. Maybe he should be looking.

But first, he had to find George.

He made a quick tour around the school building; then he walked down the hill toward the football field. The hedges would be a good hiding place for a dog, especially if he'd been hurt and was seeking shelter from the cold and the rain.

He had almost reached the stadium gates when he heard the whimper.

"George," he shouted. "Is that you?"

The dog whimpered again. It was unmistakably the sound of the shaggy red stray who had shown up on his doorstep six weeks ago and become his part-time dog.

Bending low and training his flashlight into the dark, he spotted George on the other side of the fence, huddled in a thick patch of shrubbery.

"Stay there, George. I'm coming."

He sprinted toward the padlocked gates and was halfway over the fence before he saw her—the woman from the Porsche. She was racing across the football field, her green coat unbuttoned and flapping behind her.

"Hey," he yelled.

Without breaking stride, she glanced in his direction. "I think I've found Harvey," she called. "I heard him over there." She continued running toward the bushes where Dan had spotted George.

He heard his raincoat rip as he jumped down onto the football field. Small matter. He'd patch it. What really bothered him was the disappointment that gorgeous woman would feel when she discovered she'd found the wrong dog.

He caught up with her just as she'd reached the dog.

"Oh, Harvey. You poor thing." Oblivious of the mud, she knelt beside the big dog and cradled his head.

"George." Squatting beside them, Dan addressed his dog. George acknowledged his master with a faint wag of the tail.

The woman looked up at him. "Did you say George?"

"Yes. That's my dog."

"This is not George. This is Harvey—my dog—and he looks like he's hurt." She pushed the bushes aside and bent closer to the dog. "Would you mind moving back a bit, so I can see him better?"

"If you'll step back, I'll get him out." He broke some of the larger branches trapping his dog.

The woman jerked her head up and looked him straight in the eye. "I'm a doctor. I know how to move him."

A doctor, he thought. And a bad-tempered one at that. Her big brown eyes were fairly sparkling with feeling. And he'd bet she'd never sat on a bleacher in the rain in her entire life. She was probably the symphony type.

"Allow me to help you, Doctor." He spoke with elaborate politeness that bordered on sarcasm. Fifteen minutes from now he knew he'd regret it, but he forgave himself. The death of a dream was always hard. Although it had been only a fleeting dream, he couldn't help feeling a little disappointed and somewhat cheated. She was so lovely to look at.

She smelled good, too. Even in the mud and rain, he caught the faint scent of jasmine in her hair.

They worked together for several minutes to free the big dog. When they had him out of the bushes, the doctor bent over him.

"He's weak ... probably from hunger, as well as loss of blood...." Her nimble fingers moved over the dog. "Everything seems to be okay except the back leg," she said finally. Dan could see the dog's right hind leg was a crushed mass of bloody flesh and exposed bone.

"You're a veterinarian?"

"No. A pediatrician. But I can patch him up until tomorrow morning. Then I'll take him to a vet."

"*We'll* take him to a vet," Dan countered. "It appears that George has two masters."

"Harvey." Her eyes were alight again, but this time with humor.

"Stubborn, aren't you?"

"Yes."

"My house is just up the block—the big white one with all the gingerbread trim. I'll take What's-his-name up there, and you can follow in your car."

"It's raining. We'll all go in my car."

"You'd put a wet, muddy dog in your Porsche?"

"He's not a wet, muddy dog. He's Harvey, and I love him."

Dan took in her tumbled auburn hair, her brown eyes bright with compassion. "You're not half bad, Doc," he said as he bent and carefully lifted the big dog.

"Watch his leg," she said.

Dan laughed. "Just a little bossy."

"You're not so bad yourself. Just a little—" pausing, she surveyed him from head to toe "—big."

They started across the football field toward her car.

"Dan Albany."

"Janet Hall."

"I don't know how you got over this fence, Janet...."

"I climbed, just like you."

He thought that must have been a sight to see, but he didn't say so. Dr. Janet Hall was wearing high-heeled pumps and a dress under her raincoat.

By the time they reached the fence, the rain had slowed to a drizzle.

"It's going to be tricky getting across holding this dog."

"Can you lift him over if I go first?"

Dan judged the height of the fence. "I think so, but can you hold him? He's a big dog."

"Yes." She stuck her flashlight into her pocket and smiled at him. "Have you any idea how strong a sixty-five pound child who doesn't want a shot can be? Subduing them long enough for an injection builds strength, if nothing else."

"Regular little tigers, are they?"

"Absolutely."

With her coat providing cover, she hiked her dress up matter-of-factly and found a toehold in the chain links. A hefty January breeze caught her coat and billowed it back from her body. Her legs were long and slim and lovely. As she climbed, Dan caught an intoxicating glimpse of lingerie. The doctor wore black lace under her tailored dress.

Half-embarrassed for enjoying the view so much, he turned his head away and tried to take an interest in the trees. But they were just trees, stark and bare and cold looking. Janet, on the other hand . . .

He swung his gaze back to her. She was perched astride the fence, her slip caught in the chain links.

"I seem to be stuck." Her laugh was breezy and completely unself-conscious. "If I let go to free myself, I'll lose my balance."

"Maybe I can help." He lowered George onto the grass and reached up. His hand brushed her silk-clad thigh. "Sorry."

"No problem." She'd lied, Janet thought, as Dan caught hold of her slip and tried to work it free of the fence. The problem was that she was sitting on a fence in the rain with her dress hiked up to her hips and a strange, disturbingly appealing man touching her leg. And she liked it. Ordinarily she would never be caught in such an unladylike fix. But here she was, the perfectly proper, perfectly professional Dr. Janet Hall, soaking wet, dangling her legs like a dance-hall girl and loving every minute of it. She almost wished she had stayed home and soaked her feet. Almost. If she'd stayed home she'd have missed Dan Albany's eyes. They were bright and big and incredibly blue.

A small tearing sound brought her out of her reverie.

"I'm afraid I tore your slip."

"It's okay. At least I'm not stuck anymore."

"No, you're not."

Mesmerized, she sat atop the fence and stared down at him. He seemed to be having the same problem. His hand still clutching her slip, he merely stood, gazing into her eyes.

"Well . . ." she said.

"You're getting cold."

His hand hovered briefly over her thigh, barely brushing her skin. Goose bumps rose along her leg, not entirely from the chill. It was high time to get off the fence.

Apparently Dan had come to the same conclusion. He jerked his hand back and bent over Harvey. There was no further talk as they concentrated on getting the sixty-pound dog over the fence.

"How did you get to know this big mutt?" Dan asked after they had settled in her car.

"About six weeks ago he showed up on my doorstep—on a Friday night. He looked skinny and lonesome, and he wasn't wearing a collar."

"That's just how he looked when he came to me—lonesome. I put ads in the paper, trying to find his owner. But nobody called to claim a shaggy red dog, so I took him in."

"No wonder they didn't call. He's tan. That's what my ad said."

They both laughed.

"He seemed to like being around my house all week," Dan said. "I guess it's because he loved being near the school where all the children were. But he disappeared every weekend."

"That's when he came to me. I call Harvey my weekend dog."

"And I call George my weekly dog. He's as reliable as the *Weekly Reader* the teachers use at school."

"He's a smart dog, answering to two names."

"I consider him brilliant. You ought to see the way he can sit up and beg for a steak bone."

"I never give him bones. He might get them stuck in his throat. I give him only vitamin-enriched dog food."

Dan chuckled. "That's probably the reason he spends most of his time at my house—you won't give him anything decent to eat. He's crazy about hot dogs."

"They're full of additives."

"What do you eat at ball games?"

"I never go to ball games."

He'd known it, but he'd had to ask. Strike one, he thought. But of course you couldn't rule out a woman simply because she didn't care about sports. Maybe she was the domestic type. Maybe she loved puttering around her house and kitchen. He gave her a sidelong glance. Classy. Smart. Professional. He wondered if she ever had time to putter.

He was going to ask her, but his house came into view.

Chapter Two

"Turn left here," Dan said. "That's my house."

Dan Albany's house was a revelation to Janet. On the outside it was old-fashioned and looked too large for one man. But the yard, even in its barren winter state, looked well cared for. Inside, the house smelled like bacon and coffee and cupcakes—and faintly of dirty gym socks. The front hall had an antique hall tree almost invisible under all the baseball caps, letter jackets and overcoats. To this collection, Dan added his umbrella and raincoat. Janet feared the tree might topple under the weight.

He picked up the dog again and led the way to his den. A fire was going in the fireplace and two Victorian lamps made soft pools of light in the darkness. The room was filled with large, comfortable-looking furniture and lots of clutter. It had the lived-in look of a man who collects things but doesn't quite know where to put them. An antique carousel music box shared space on an end table with a signed baseball, an old papier-mâché duck decoy and a letter opener.

Hand-crocheted doilies, all in different designs, decorated the arms of all the chairs. A child's wooden rocking horse sat in front of the bookshelves, which were fairly groaning under their load of books and knickknacks.

Janet had never been in a room quite so astonishingly cluttered. It wasn't dirty or even messy, just jumbled.

Dan placed the dog on a rug in front of the fireplace, and Janet had no more time to consider his house. She patched Harvey the best way she could while Dan held him steady. She liked the way he constantly stroked the dog and spoke soothing words to him.

"You're good," she said, looking up into those amazing eyes. "There are days I could use you at the clinic." She began to pack her medical supplies into her black bag.

"I love children and animals." Dan gave George one last pat, then moved to stand beside the mantel as the dog's head sagged and his eyes closed in sleep. He watched the play of firelight in Janet's hair as she bent over her bag. Nice. "If we're both going to be involved with this dog, I think we should decide what to call him. No use in him having to remember two names."

"I'm partial to Harvey."

"Any reason?"

"It's the name of a favorite uncle of mine."

Dan smiled. "He doesn't mind being godfather to a dog?"

"He wouldn't, if he knew. He was crazy about animals. I think word got out among strays, because he never had fewer than six dogs at a time." She snapped her bag shut and stood up. "He died five years ago."

"I'm sorry."

"So am I."

"Then we'll call him Harvey."

"Thank you."

"You're more than welcome."

Lulled by the cozy firelight and the easy, relaxed manner of Dan Albany, Janet felt like sliding into one of the big, fat chairs and leaning her head back. A woman could get addicted to a cozy room like this. But she couldn't afford such addictions.

"Could you direct me to your bathroom?" she said. "I need to wash up before I go."

"Down the hall, then through the door on the left."

When Janet got into the bathroom, she suddenly realized how tense she was. Today she had admitted little Randy Sanderford to the hospital. Scizures. And he was only six years old. His mother had been in tears and his father hadn't been much better. Seeing the fragile-looking little boy lying against the white sheets, she'd wanted to cry herself; but she had to be strong. Always, she had to be strong for her patients as well as herself. The compassion she felt had to be tempered with discipline. Her work demanded it.

She leaned briefly against the sink, then straightened her shoulders and scrubbed her hands. She'd check on Harvey one last time; then she'd go home and climb into a hot bath with a stack of medical journals. Much of her professional reading was done in the tub. Doing two things at once was the only way she could make enough time in her day for all the things that needed attention.

The den was empty except for Harvey. Janet knelt beside him.

"You're back." Dan Albany spoke from the doorway.

"Yes. I thought I'd check on Harvey before I leave."

"I made hot chocolate." He held out two steaming mugs. "And don't say you don't have time."

"That's exactly what I was going to say. How did you know?"

"I've been around high-powered people enough to know." He came into the room, walking carefully so the chocolate wouldn't slosh over the brims. "Why don't you take that rocking chair beside the fire?"

As Janet moved to the chair, she couldn't help smiling. Big men looked so innocent when they were trying to be careful. Removing her coat and silk scarf, she leaned back in the chair. It made a rocking motion as if it knew exactly what to do. The feeling was so pleasant she continued rocking, stopping only long enough to take the cup from Dan.

Her hand brushed against his, and for a second time that evening she felt a shock of awareness. She could think of absolutely no scientific reason why touching Dan Albany should make shivers run along her spine. Strange. She knew nothing about the man except that he loved dogs and had a cluttered house. She decided to find out more.

As he settled into the chair opposite her, she took a sip of chocolate. "Your wife must stay awfully busy dusting all this... memorabilia." She'd stopped herself just in time to keep from saying "junk." Great. She was about as subtle as an elephant dancing on a soufflé.

His laugh was a happy roar that made the room seem brighter. "I'm not married, Doctor. Are you?"

"I didn't mean to...well, of course, I shouldn't have..." She took a long, fortifying drink of hot chocolate. "I don't have time for marriage."

That statement—and the stiff-lipped way she said it—told Dan about all he needed to know. Dr. Janet Hall was definitely not a sweet, old-fashioned woman. And yet she looked so right beside his fire....

He repented his wicked, teasing ways and smiled at her. "I do the dusting myself, such as it is. But if I had a wife, she'd have nothing to do but dust and pamper me—and all the children."

"Children?"

"About a hundred and twenty-five of them—each one special. They're not mine, of course, except when they're at school."

"You're a teacher, then?"

"Yes. Graden Junior High. Math."

Math, Janet thought. She perked up. Here was a man who at least understood the scientific mind, even if his house was a wreck.

"Of course," Dan added, "my first love is coaching."

"You're a coach?"

"Yes, soccer." Dan leaned forward in his chair. "Do you think I'll live, Doc?"

"What?"

He chuckled. "You looked so disconcerted that I couldn't resist teasing you. It's an old habit of mine. Comes from growing up in a large family. We were always kidding and carrying on with each other."

"A large family must be nice."

"I think so. Someday I'm going to have one myself." He lifted the cup to his lips and watched her over the brim. Such elegant bone structure. Too bad she was a doctor. Still . . . "Of course, I have to find the right woman first."

"I suppose you have all sorts of requirements. Most men do."

Auburn hair would be nice, he thought as he watched the firelight play in hers. Brown eyes, too. Funny, he'd never thought about the color of his dream woman's hair and eyes. He smiled at her.

"Do you knit, Janet?"

"I beg your pardon?"

"Knit. You know . . . make blankets and sweaters and things with yarn and those long needles that click."

"Goodness, no. I don't have time to knit."

"I'll bet you love to putter in the yard."

"My yard is about three times bigger than this tea-cup...thank goodness," she said.

"You're probably the type who loves to relax by baking cookies on a cold, rainy day."

Janet set her cup on the table beside the rocking chair and laughed. Dan Albany was being about as subtle as she had been. She didn't know why that should make her suddenly feel so good.

"I don't bake, I don't knit and I don't putter. Any other specifications, Dan Albany?"

He laughed. "You caught me red-handed, Doc. I find myself attracted to you, and yet you're the exact opposite of everything I've ever thought I wanted in a woman."

The silence stretched between them as they studied each other across the firelit room. She thought he was big and bold and hopelessly old-fashioned, and she knew beyond a shadow of a doubt that he spelled trouble.

He thought she was vibrant and beautiful and ridiculously modern, and he was positive she'd turn his world upside down. It was best to put a stop to the battle before a war got started. He decided that the quickest way was to use the big artillery.

Leaning back in his chair, he dropped the first bomb. "You're absolutely not my type, at all."

Janet's back stiffened. Every good impression she'd had about Dan Albany disappeared. Call it ego, call it over-work, call it any darned thing—she was insulted straight to the core by the arrogance of this man.

"I wasn't auditioning for the part."

"Are you angry, Doc?"

"Angry? Why should I be angry?" She stood up so fast that the rocking chair kept rocking. "A soccer coach says I'm not his type. I should feel honored."

"A soccer coach?" Underneath the low-voiced question were the rattling of sabers and the sounding of the battle cry.

She answered by firing a volley. "Excuse me. I should have said chauvinistic soccer coach."

He put down his cup and stood up with the slow grace of a born athlete. Although his movements were easy, his body gave the appearance of being wired for explosion. "Have you finished with the scientific analysis, Doctor?"

"Not yet. Any man who expects only to have his furniture dusted and his ego pampered doesn't deserve a good woman."

"I expect more." He advanced toward her, war flags flying above the battlements. "Much, much more."

He was directly in front of her now, standing so close she could feel his body heat. She braced herself against the chair.

"Of course," she said. "I forgot the baking and knitting and puttering."

"You forgot this." He caught her shoulders, fully intending to pull her into his arms and show her a thing or two about chauvinistic soccer coaches. But something stopped him. Perhaps it was the way she looked at him, the eyes widened just slightly—but not with fear. Instinctively he knew he was holding a woman who wouldn't back down from the devil. The idea pleased him enormously.

He gazed deep into her eyes, mesmerized by the challenge he saw there. No woman had ever made him feel quite so... he didn't know any words to describe the way he felt. All he knew was that something warm unfurled inside him and he wanted to touch her, to feel the texture of her skin.

He lifted one hand and cupped her cheek.

Janet forced herself to stand stiffly. There was absolutely no logical reason to feel the way she was feeling right now. He was just a man, and that was merely a hand on her face, she reasoned. But all the logic in the world didn't stop her pulse from quickening.

His hand trailed across her cheek and gently traced the outline of her lips. Her nerve endings screamed, and a strange heat built in her body. Diagnosis—temporary insanity. Prognosis—curable. But not at the moment. For now she could do nothing but surrender to the persuasive power of Dan Albany.

It was a small victory for Dan, and he pressed his advantage. He slid his hand back along her cheek and into her hair, that wine-rich hair that had beckoned him all evening. Catching the nape of her neck, he gently urged her forward and leaned closer until their lips were almost touching.

She'd thought him big and bold and hopelessly old-fashioned. Now she added dangerous to his catalogue of sins. He made her think of cozy firelit evenings when the touch of a hand is magic. He made her consider passionate nights in a brass bed with rain tap-dancing on the roof and love flowing richly through the blood. He made her dream of orange blossoms and a nursery decorated in pink and blue.

She must be going mad. She decided to quit while she still could.

Janet raised her hands and pushed against his chest. He released her immediately and leaned casually against the mantel as if nothing out of the ordinary had happened.

"You've just proved my point, Coach. Only a man with a gigantic ego would manhandle a woman he barely met."

"I call it touching, Janet." His smile was slow and easy. "And you accepted it."

"I had no choice."

"You enjoyed it."

"Like hell."

"Ladies don't cuss."

"Add that to my list of shortcomings. I'm no lady."

"Did you know that your hair looks like burgundy wine in the firelight?"

"Only a man of your supreme arrogance would believe that praising a woman's looks excuses odious behavior." Turning her back to him, Janet jerked her coat off the chair.

Dan left the mantel and stood behind her. "Allow me." His big hands covered hers.

"I don't need your help, thank you very much."

"My mama taught me that a gentleman always helps a lady with her coat—no matter how unladylike she acts." He unceremoniously bundled her into the green raincoat.

"A pity your mama didn't teach you anything about subtlety."

"She tried. I guess I'm a slow learner."

Catching her shoulders, Dan turned her around. She was furious, and justifiably so he thought as he looked down at her. He experienced a moment of regret that he had so quickly destroyed the easy camaraderie between them. Not even telling himself it was all for the best could ease his conscience. But what was done, was done.

"What are you planning now?" she asked. "Another demonstration of your superior strength?"

"I'm going to button your coat. You can't go out in the cold like that." His fingers brushed lightly under her chin as he fastened the top button.

Janet briefly considered fighting, then decided there was more to be gained by submission. She'd be damned if she'd give him the satisfaction of knowing what his touch did to her.

He handled the buttons with ease, as if performing a chore he'd done many times before. He probably did this every day for dozens of women, she thought—all of them no doubt sitting at home right now, baking gingerbread and knitting afghans and hoping he would call. She hoped they all got high cholesterol from eating hot dogs.

Two buttons down and two to go. She held her breath.

"Did you know your eyes turn gold in the center when you're angry?"

She glanced up at him and then wished she hadn't. Up close he was even more devastatingly delicious. And so totally unsuitable. She had to keep telling herself that.

"There's nothing mysterious about the color of a person's eyes. It's merely a matter of genes."

"In your case, it's magic."

His hands moved to the button over her breasts. Janet fought to keep from sucking in her breath. Even through all her layers of clothing, she was astonishingly aware of his touch. A slow, lazy smile curved his lips. He *knew*, damn him.

"Magic," he said again, so softly she barely heard him.

"There's no need for two of us to go to the vet," Janet said, trying to regain control through some conversation. "I'll come by in the morning after my hospital rounds and pick up Harvey."

"What time will you be finished?" His hands lingered over the button. She wanted to scream.

"Nine."

"Good. I'll bring Harvey and pick you up at the hospital."

"No."

His hands were still on her, one inside her coat and one outside, not fastening the button, not doing *anything*, just hovering there like two giant flatirons. She was getting hot.

"Why not?"

"It's perfectly ridiculous—a waste of time. One person should be able to take care of Harvey. It's more efficient that way."

"Is efficiency one of your top priorities?"

Why didn't he move his hand? She took a deep breath. "Yes. But that's probably something you wouldn't understand."

"Being a coach?"

"I didn't say that."

What was happening? he wondered. He'd meant to drop a bomb and end it all, nice and quick and clean. No futile speculations, no useless dreams of turning the beautiful doctor into a hearth-warming homebody. Instead he found himself lingering over the simple pleasure of buttoning her coat.

And she kept baiting him, dammit. He smiled as he took hold of the last button. Of course, he was also baiting her. It seemed that the coach and the doctor were destined to do battle. He felt invigorated, challenged—and he was definitely looking forward to their next skirmish.

He fastened the last button on her coat, then reached and caught her shoulders. "I suppose we could debate the issue all night," he said.

"If you think I'm staying here all night, you're crazy."

"I don't want you here all night."

"Then why are you hanging onto me?"

He merely tightened his hold and smiled. "Game tactics. I don't want you leaving the field until I've scored my point."

"You should know something about me, Coach Albany. I never quit the field."

"Neither do I." He reached to turn her collar up around her face. Except for the deepening of her color, she didn't show any sign of emotion. "Since you're obviously too stubborn to give in to my way..."

"I am not..."

"... and I'm definitely too bullheaded to do things your way, we'll compromise."

"That's the first sensible thing you've said all evening."

"I have my moments."

She wished he hadn't smiled again. His smile compensated for a multitude of sins.

"I'll bring Harvey and meet you at the vet's. That way we're both spared spending unnecessary time in each other's company."

"Agreed." Janet ducked out of his grasp and reached for her medical bag. "Good night, Coach."

"See you tomorrow, Doc."

He took her arm to escort her out.

"Don't bother," she said. "I can find my way."

"I insist. My early childhood training in manners, you know." Chuckling, he opened the front door.

His laughter followed Janet all the way down the steps and to her car. It was still echoing in her thoughts when she reached her condominium. Willing herself to forget, she pulled off her muddy clothes, drew her bath, climbed into the tub and picked up a medical journal. The article she was looking for had been written by a colleague of hers, Dr. Glen Rikert. She read two paragraphs, then gave up and leaned her head against her plastic bath pillow. Scoliosis couldn't hold a candle to Coach Dan Albany.

"Damned arrogant rogue."

Chapter Three

Dan rose at 5:00 a.m. on Saturday, as he did every morning. Like any well-trained athlete, he kept his body in superb condition with a strict regimen of exercise. Diet, he fudged on. He had a fondness for junk food, and so far his body hadn't suffered. He didn't believe half those horror stories put out by the doctors anyhow. A little pizza for breakfast never hurt anybody.

After polishing off half a pizza, he went into the den to check on Harvey. When he neared the fireplace, he noticed Janet's green silk scarf lying on the rocking chair. He picked it up and let the silky material drift through his fingers. Her scent clung there. Jasmine. Such an old-fashioned, beautiful fragrance. Without thinking he put the scarf to his nose and inhaled.

Harvey whined.

Grinning sheepishly, Dan threw the scarf back onto the rocker and knelt beside the dog. "Sometimes old men get foolish fancies, don't we, boy?'' He rubbed the dog's head. ''How are you feeling this morning? Up to breakfast?''

When he'd managed to get Harvey to eat a few bites of cold hot dog, Dan left for a brisk five-mile run. He returned feeling invigorated and ready for anything—even the ridiculously modern Dr. Hall.

Whistling, he bundled Harvey into his pickup truck and headed to the veterinarian.

Janet was waiting for him at the vet's office, wearing an expensive suit and classic pumps. Perfectly correct dress for a doctor. She probably wore the pumps to bed. The thought gave him a perverse sort of satisfaction.

''Good morning, Doc.''

''Good morning, Coach.''

The labels made clear exactly where they stood, Dan thought, as they had last night—on opposite sides of the battlefield.

''I've already signed Harvey in,'' Janet said. ''The receptionist should be calling his name soon.'' Dan watched her move toward him with that lovely fluid grace he'd noticed last night. She put her hand on Harvey's head. ''How are you, boy?'' She bent closer and scratched under the dog's chin. ''Feeling better? That's a good boy.'' The dog's tail wagged feebly.

''Quite a bedside manner you've got there, Doc.''

''Would it surprise you to know it's not a manner? It's real feeling.''

''Not in the least. I believe last night proved you have feeling.''

The memory of his touch burned through her. Janet unbuttoned her wool suit jacket to let some of the heat escape. ''It won't happen again,'' she assured him.

Although he was absolutely positive she was wrong for him, he hated being dismissed by her. "We'll see," he said. He figured it was his male pride talking.

She figured it was his ego. "You need to practice your technique, Coach. Caveman tactics are out of style."

"Not if they work."

Two minutes together and they were already battling up a storm. Dan didn't know why, but he hadn't enjoyed a Saturday morning so much in a long, long time.

Before Janet could reply, the receptionist called her name. "Dr. Hall? You can bring Harvey back."

"I'll carry him," Dan said.

"Fine. Let's go."

Together they walked toward the receptionist. Billie Jean Haskins, her name tag read. She was young and vivacious and bleached blond and trying very hard to make a good impression on her first day of work. She'd thought that Dr. Janet Hall was beautiful but remote in a cool, professional sort of way. It surprised her to notice that Dr. Hall had managed to land a man who seemed so...casual. His hair was windblown, his shirt was open at the throat, and his jeans were comfortably faded. He was the most devastating man Billie Jean had ever seen. She decided she could earn Brownie points with the high-class doctor by complimenting her on her taste in men.

"My, my, Dr. Hall, I must say that there's not a man in Tupelo to equal your husband."

"He's not my husband—"

"We're not married—"

Janet and Dan spoke at the same time. Their denial was so vehement that Billie Jean was taken aback. She attempted to correct her mistake.

"Well, I just naturally assumed that he belonged to you, the two of you being so familiar and all. I mean, the way you were arguing a while ago, I just knew you were husband and wife.'' Oh, Lord, she thought. Now look what she'd said. She'd only made matters worse. The doctor and that gorgeous man both looked as if they were about to explode.

''We weren't arguing—''

''We were just discussing—''

Janet and Dan looked at each other. He was the first to laugh. It started as a muffled chuckle and grew to a full-bodied roar of mirth. Janet joined him.

Billie Jean thought they were crazy. Besides that, they had made her wonder if she'd chosen the right job. Maybe she should have stuck to hairdressing the way her sister had advised her. But what did Mildred Ann know anyway? Billie Jean heaved a big sigh. Life was so tangled up it was a wonder anybody could get through without going loony.

''If you'll follow me, I'll take you back to Dr. Bailey.'' She turned away from them and started down the hall toward the examining rooms.

Dan looked at the receptionist's stiff back and proud little chin. He hurried forward and fell in step beside her. ''It was a natural mistake, honey. Please don't think you offended us.'' The only thing that had offended him was Janet's vehement denial that they were married. She thought he was that unsuitable, did she?

Seeing Billie Jean's obvious discomfort, Janet sought to reassure her. She caught up to them and patted Billie Jean's arm. ''It's all right, Billie Jean. Anyone might have made that mistake. I'm certainly not upset.'' Except at Dan Albany. He thought she was that wrong for him, did he?

She'd show him.

He'd show her.

Both tall people, Dan and Janet looked at each other across the top of Billie Jean's head. He saw the wicked sparkle in her eye and she saw the determined light in his.

If she knew what was good for her, she'd never see him again.

If he had any sense he'd run like hell.

The drumbeat of their steps punctuated his thoughts as they marched down the tiled hallway. When they reached the examining room, the strong smell of antiseptic wafted through the open door.

He barely noticed.

Dan bowed from the waist. "After you."

Janet thought he looked absurd, holding that big dog and bowing like some seventeenth-century cavalier, especially when she already knew he had no manners at all. Absurd, but charming in an offbeat way.

She gave him her most flirtatious smile. At least, she hoped it was flirtatious. Since it hadn't been used since the Dark Ages, she couldn't be sure. "How gallant. Thank you, kind sir."

Dan thought that smile looked as false as his Great-aunt Hettie's teeth. False but cute in a funny, heart-tugging kind of way.

The veterinarian paid their odd behavior no attention. He was no doubt used to all kinds.

Suddenly aware of Dr. Bailey, they stopped their game long enough to tell him about Harvey. On the examining table the dog looked up at his two owners with mournful eyes, but his tail never stopped its weak wagging.

"He's gritty, isn't he?" Dr. Bailey said. "That wound looks as if it's old, at least a week, and yet he's in surprisingly good shape."

"He's a fighter," Dan said.

Janet knew the dog was a fighter, but she also knew that his wound was quite serious. "What's the prognosis, Dr. Bailey?"

"There is a lot of infection. I'll try to save the leg, but I won't know for a few days. I'll need to keep him here, of course." He smiled at them. "He's in good hands, and you can come to visit whenever you wish. No set visiting hours."

Janet and Dan said their goodbyes to Harvey and left the office, both so busy with their plans that they barely noticed each other as they walked across the parking lot to their cars.

When she reached her Porsche, Janet turned to Dan. "Do you have a busy day planned?"

"Soccer practice this afternoon."

She didn't want to tip her hand by asking where. She merely nodded and smiled.

"And you?" He opened the car door for her.

"I'm not on call this weekend. I'm going to enjoy the wicked pleasures of pampering myself all day, and tonight I'm going to indulge in the ballet." Idle chatter, she thought, but it gave her time to assess her opponent. She slid into the front seat and treated him to another of her flirty smiles. She fancied she was getting better with practice. "Take care."

"You, too."

He gave her a small salute, then got into his old Ford pickup. It looked even more battered parked there beside her shiny sports car. Never mind, he thought. Appearances could be deceiving. Never judge a warrior by his battle gear. Chuckling, he turned the key and backed out of the lot. Janet, just in front of him, tooted her horn and waved.

The first thing he did when he got home was look up her address in the telephone book. He didn't know how he had managed to see her twice and still not know where she lived.

His fingers traced the Hs until he found her. Those ritzy condos on the corner of Jefferson and Madison. He should have known. He was not discouraged, however. When a man sets out to prove to a woman that he is God's answer to her prayers, nothing will stand in his way.

Grinning, he put the telephone book back onto his cluttered desk and picked up the newspaper. Ignoring the sports, he flipped to the entertainment section. The Atlanta Ballet was in town. That had to be it. Gritting his teeth, he picked up the phone and ordered a ticket. He half hoped the girl on the other end of the line would say, "Sorry, we're sold out." But she didn't. She said his ticket would be waiting at the door.

He stood and stretched. It was a good thing he had soccer practice this afternoon. All that exercise and fresh air might prepare him for an evening of puny music that sounded like it was squeezed through a plastic straw and grown men cavorting around in tight silk britches.

He went into the hall and plucked his favorite baseball cap off the hall tree. God, Doc was cute when she tried to flirt.

Janet had friends in high places. In the blue-and-peach comfort of her condo, she called her friend Michelle Leonard, principal of Graden Junior High.

"Michelle, this is Janet."

"Hi. I haven't heard from you in an age. You're still busy trying to find a cure for every disease known to man, I guess."

"Something like that." Janet crossed her fingers and took the plunge. "You have a teacher at your school, a Dan Albany..."

"You know Dan!"

"Not really. We just met."

"He's a sweetheart, Janet. Dedicated, sincere, friendly, charming..."

Janet burst out laughing. "Stop the hard sell, Michelle. I'm not planning on buying him."

"Then what are you going to do with him? Try to get him to the altar like half the women in Tupelo?"

"Wrong. I'm planning to teach him a lesson."

"Janet! It's been four years since Guy Maxwell, and now you tell me all you have in mind for Dan is to teach him a lesson? Don't ruin my Saturday."

"It's been only three years," Janet corrected her friend, "and I won't belabor you with the sordid details of my plan. Just tell me one thing."

"What?"

"Where and when does Dan Albany have soccer practice?"

"Aha."

"What does 'aha' mean?"

"Nothing. Just thinking out loud."

"Michelle..."

"All right. Two o'clock. The practice field on the south side of the school."

"How long will the practice last?"

"Dan usually keeps the kids an hour, sometimes just a bit longer. Janet... what in this world are you going to do?"

"Play it by ear, Michelle. We'll have lunch soon, and I'll tell you all about it."

"We've been trying to have lunch together since November."

"This time we'll make it work. Thanks, Michelle."

When Janet hung up she was smiling. Dan was in for quite a surprise. Gracious, he was cute when he tried to be gallant.

Janet waited until 2:45, then bundled herself into her mittens and heavy parka. The soccer field was just a block down the street from her. She could walk it in a few minutes.

Before she went outside, she drank a big glass of orange juice. Vitamin C. With her heavy work schedule she couldn't afford to come down with a cold.

She pulled up her hood and started down the street.

Dan saw her coming. She was wearing enough clothes to outfit an expedition to the frozen tundra. But even under all the clothes there was no mistaking the dark red hair that escaped her hood and the fluid, gliding way she had of moving.

He hastily lined his team up for practice kicks into the goal; then he went to meet her at the side of the field.

"Janet. Fancy seeing you here."

"Just out for an afternoon stroll." She slapped her mittens together to keep the circulation going in her hands.

Dan could barely keep from laughing out loud. She was no more out for a stroll than he was a polka-dot elephant. For some unknown reason, she had come to see him. He was inordinately pleased by the idea. And he could hardly wait to see what she was up to.

"What a coincidence that you happened to walk this way. I'm just finishing soccer practice."

"Really? How fascinating."

Her eyes got darker when she lied and her nose wrinkled up. He had a hard time keeping from reaching up to touch that pert little nose.

"I'd be glad for you to watch the practice. Unfortunately, the boys will be leaving in about five minutes."

She looked crestfallen. "Oh, that's too bad. I would so love to learn more about the game."

He wasn't fooled; he was merely fascinated. "You would?"

"Yes. I used to play some with my brother...." She'd allowed Brett to bully her into one game when she was sixteen and he was fourteen. One smart kick on the shin, and she'd quit the field. Her soccer experience had lasted a total of three minutes. "That was many years ago, of course, when we were both young." She watched Dan closely to see how well he was buying her story. She couldn't tell. All she could tell was that he looked delicious in his navy sweats. "I'm a little rusty on the rules."

The unspoken invitation was so obvious that only a fool would have missed it. "Make me an offer," she was saying. Although Dan had known he'd take her on the field the minute he saw her walking down the street, he decided to play with her a while longer.

"The encyclopedias have excellent descriptions of the game. Most of them even have diagrams of the fields."

"Well...yes..." She flashed him a provocative smile. She was getting better at flirting, he noticed. "But it seems such a shame to waste a sunny day like today sitting inside reading an encyclopedia."

"The library has some great books on soccer, too. I'll recommend some that you can check out and save for a rainy day."

She could have strangled him. "That's a grand idea. Still..." She paused and looked into the sky, shading her hand against the sun. "It's such a beautiful day." If he didn't take that hint, she guessed she'd have to ask him point blank.

Dan decided to put her out of her agony. "I have a wonderful idea."

"You do?"

"Since you're here and I'm almost finished with practice, why don't I give you a few pointers?"

"You'd do that for me?"

He loved her imitation of a wide-eyed innocent. But there was absolutely nothing innocent about the wicked gleam in her eyes and the provocative way she stood.

He grinned. "You're going to love this private lesson, Doc."

He took her hand and led her onto the playing field. His team of thirteen-year-olds crowded around to be introduced. Afterward, she waited while he talked with them about their next game.

He was good with children. That was the first thing she noticed. The next was that the children not only respected him, they loved him. Watching Dan with his team, she knew she was watching something rare and beautiful. At that moment the crack in her armor widened until it was a gaping hole. She was vulnerable.

But she couldn't quit now. She was committed. One man had already dismissed her as too busy and too dedicated to her career for marriage. She'd be damned if another would do the same.

Finally the last of the soccer team left the field, and she was alone with Dan. His incredible blue eyes raked her from head to toe.

"You're wearing too many clothes."

"I beg your pardon?" She pulled her hood tighter around her face.

"I said, you're wearing too many clothes. You need to take some of them off."

"For what?"

"Soccer." He grinned at her. "You weren't thinking of something else, were you, Doc?"

"Of course not."

"Good. Neither was I." He reached out and began to unbutton her coat.

"What do you think you're doing?"

"Habit. Good manners, you know. Helping ladies on and off with their coats."

Just in time, she remembered her purpose and bit back a sharp retort.

"Thank you."

"You're welcome." He slid the heavy wool parka over her shoulders and tossed it on one of the wooden benches that lined the field. Then he caught the tail of his sweatshirt and stripped it over his head. Underneath he was wearing a flannel shirt. "Here. Put this on. It's lightweight, but it's designed to keep out the cold."

The shirt was still warm from his body. It also smelled faintly of him, a clean, spicy, soap smell. She hugged her arms around her torso, pulling his warmth closer.

"Cold?"

"No. Just adjusting the shirt." She began to smooth down the tail. "It's a little big."

"It's never looked so good. Are you ready for your first lesson?"

"Yes."

"Good. Then listen closely, Doc."

Listen? That wasn't exactly what she had in mind. She sat down on the bench and waited. She saw the very devil dancing in his eyes as he propped one foot on the bench and began a long-winded technical lecture that would have bored the pants off even the staunchest soccer fan.

If he thought he was going to get the best of her, he was sadly mistaken. She called on all the powers of her scientific mind to listen.

When he had finished the lecture, he grinned at her. "Did you get that part about fouling?"

"Yes. If a player fouls, the opponents can be awarded a direct free kick, a penalty kick or an indirect free kick."

He was impressed. "And do you remember the size of the playing field? That's very important."

"In international competition the field may be one hundred ten to one hundred twenty yards long, and the width may extend from seventy to eighty yards. The field is the same length in college competition in the U.S., but the width can be sixty-five to seventy-five yards wide. Anything else, Coach?"

"That's amazing."

"I'm a fast learner."

"Then I'd say you're more than ready to play."

Tossing her mittens onto the bench, she smiled at him. "I'm equal to whatever play you have in mind."

Dan watched her sashay toward the goal line. She had spunk. He'd always admired that in a woman. Of course, she wasn't really interested in soccer. She was simply playing a cat-and-mouse game with him. And he was happy to oblige. It fit right into his own game plan.

He tossed the ball onto the field. "Defend your goal, Doc."

He dribbled the ball expertly toward the goal, using fancy footwork designed to show off his skills. He knew he was grandstanding, but he wasn't above such tactics. When the stakes were this high, anything was fair.

She ran toward him and tried to kick the ball away. Her toe connected with his shin. He could have easily dribbled around her and gotten a clean shot at the goal; but he hedged, enjoying the sight of her trying to act as if she liked the game.

She was hopelessly inept, and within three minutes she'd peppered his leg from ankle to knee with kicks. He thought briefly of his pads lying on the front seat of his car. It was just his luck that he'd chosen this practice session not to wear them. He'd have a few bruises, but that was a small price for victory.

Suddenly he pulled away from her, sending the ball racing down the field in front of his expert feet. He drew back his foot. The ball arced in the air and landed between the goalposts with a loud thunk.

"Beautiful," Janet called.

He turned and started running toward her. "Not half as beautiful as you."

Before she knew what was happening, he had tackled her. He hit the ground first, breaking her fall.

Her face was pressed against his broad chest and her legs were tangled with his. She raised herself on her elbows and stared down at him. "I didn't know tackling was a part of soccer."

"This is a new game." Holding her around the waist, he rolled over, pinning her underneath him. He was smiling. "The name of this game is Truth."

"Truth?" Before she had come to the soccer field, she had counted on being completely in control. Somehow Dan had managed to wrest control from her. It was time to leave and regroup. She squirmed under him, testing her possibilities of escape. That was a mistake. He was stretched full length on top of her, and her move made her stunningly aware of every inch of him.

He smoothed back her tumbled hair. "Yes. Truth. You can start by telling me why you're here." His voice had gone husky.

Ah, but he was clever, she thought. And she liked it. She'd have been disappointed to find he wasn't a worthy opponent. And his hand on her face. She closed her eyes and reveled in his touch. She'd never known a man's hands could be so gentle and yet so persuasive. It felt as if her bones melted under his touch. Scientifically, she knew that couldn't happen, but it did.

She weighed her options. She could lie to him, but he'd never believe it. She'd have to change her game plan—advance the action, so to speak.

Dropping her voice to a seductive purr, she looked straight into his blue eyes. "Don't you know why I came?"

He bent so close his breath stirred the hair at her temple. "For this?"

His mouth took possession of hers. Ever so gently he tasted, taking his time, savoring the sweetness. The slow, tender persuasion of his kiss made her senses reel. She'd expected harshness and domination. Dan Albany kept surprising her.

Subtly his weight shifted. It was impossible not to notice how perfectly they fit together. And how right he felt. Ahh, he was dangerous. And she was falling, falling into the delicate trap he had set. A little while longer and she would pull herself free. She reached for his head and wound her fingers into his hair.

"Hmm." She didn't know if she had made the sound of contentment or if he had. No matter. The kiss was sweet anesthesia. They were both going under.

Dan had meant to make the kiss swift and hard and quick. He'd meant to prove his domination and send her on her way, wiser and more cautious and aching for more. Instead, he was the one aching for more.

He rolled to his side, taking her with him, never losing contact with her mouth. Ahh, she was delicious. And so giving. A great tenderness got mixed up with the passion so that he found himself gently rocking her in his arms. This had to stop.

He savored her a small eternity longer, then drew back and looked into her eyes. It took great effort to remember that they were only playing a game.

"Did you get what you came for, Doc?"

"Is that a victory chortle I hear, Coach?"

"Yes."

She moved so close to him that she could feel the buttons on his flannel shirt pressing into her chest, even through the sweatshirt.

"It's a little early for a celebration. I haven't quit the field yet."

Pressing her mouth against his, she began her assault.

Chapter Four

Her lips stroked across his, as sugary sweet and deliciously soft as the inside of cream-filled cupcakes. His hands glided into the silky curls at the nape of her neck and urged her closer. Drugged by the sweet wine of her kisses, he forgot that he was playing a game, forgot that his was the victory. Time and place spun away, and reality came to him in fragmented impressions. Rich burgundy hair brushing against his cheek, soft and satiny as the brocade on his sister's wedding dress. Delightful swell of breasts, pressed so close their heartbeats tangled. Hips, deliciously trim and firm, pressed hotly against his.

He couldn't get enough. His hands began to move, tracing her body, murmuring over her with the soft tenderness of a love song.

A languor stole over her. Where was the victory? she wondered. Where was the sense of conquering the enemy, vanquishing the opponent? His hands played over her like butterflies dancing in the hot summer sun. It couldn't be

January. They couldn't be lying on the hard cold ground of the soccer field. Some trick had transported them to Eden. She was woman; he was man. She was his Eve; he was her Adam. Together they were discovering romance.

Her last thought was so shocking it almost brought her to her senses. Almost, but not quite. Her very own Adam chose that moment to delve into the rich softness of her mouth. The deep, even strokes of his tongue sent wildfire racing through her blood. She would stay a while longer; she *had* to stay a while longer, long enough to memorize the rich, hot taste of him, the warm, hard feel of him, the clean, masculine smell of him.

She drank deeply of him, and when she finally could she pulled out of his embrace.

"Quitting the field so soon, Doc?" His mouth was only inches from hers and his breath fanned her hot face.

"Not quitting the field." She stood up on legs that were as wobbly and uncertain as her voice. Looking down at him, she managed a triumphant smile. "Just quitting while I'm ahead."

"You are?" He rose with easy grace and cupped her face, turning it this way and that, studying her with the thoroughness she used on bacteria under a microscope. Her color was high, the flushed pink on cream of a Rubens painting. "Is that a blush I see?"

"No. It's the flush of victory."

"You won, did you?" His eyes crinkled at the corners with amusement.

"I think I proved my point rather nicely." She pulled out of his grasp and walked to the nearby bench. Picking up her wool parka, she turned to face him again. "When I want to, I can definitely be your type. Good day, Coach."

She walked quickly away, triumphant in her victory, totally unaware that she was still wearing his sweatshirt.

He watched her until she was out of sight. Then he gathered up the soccer balls and sprinted to his pickup truck. Without his sweatshirt and her body heat, he was suddenly cold. He turned on the key and let the motor run, blowing on his hands to warm them until his heater could kick in and take away the chill.

Snatches of old country-and-western love songs came to him, and he began to sing in his loud but passable baritone. A couple of his students, chasing their dog down the sidewalk, heard him singing and stopped to yell, "Hey, Coach. What'cha doin'?"

Grinning, he rolled his window down a notch. "Just practicing, boys."

They giggled and waved and gave chase to their dog again.

Dan put his truck into gear and headed home. He had a lot to do before evening. If Doc thought she'd proved herself to be his type, just wait till he got through proving himself to be *her* type.

By the time Janet got back to her condo she had rationalized the encounter on the soccer field to put herself in the best possible light. The kiss had definitely been her trump card, she thought as she pushed open her door. She'd noticed Dan's heavy, erratic heartbeat, his ragged, uneven breathing. Yes, she'd definitely disturbed the coach. That meant her plan was working.

She stripped off her wool parka and saw Dan's sweatshirt. Good heavens. She'd walked off the soccer field in such a haze of passion that she'd forgotten to give him back his shirt. Some victory. He must be laughing his head off.

She certainly wasn't going to take the sweatshirt back now. That would only prove to him that she'd carried it off by mistake in the first place. Her best plan would be to return it and act as if she'd meant to keep it all along.

Taking a hanger from her closet, she carefully hung up her parka; then she started to strip Dan's shirt over her head. The minute her fingers sank into the soft material, she thought of him, the hard, muscular lines of his body, the heady nectar of his kiss, the gentle murmuring caresses of his hands.

She'd wear the shirt a while longer. After all, it was an extraordinarily chilly day. Humming an aria from Puccini's *Madame Butterfly*, she got her bottle of lemon wax and began to polish her immaculate furniture.

By evening Dan had worked himself into a sweat trying to match his paltry collection of shirts and ties to his one good wool suit. His Sunday suit, he called it. It was seldom worn and hopelessly out of style and certainly not *his* style, but he kept it around for funerals and weddings and graduations. A man in his position couldn't afford to be entirely suitless.

He finally settled on a pale pink oxford shirt and a classic red-striped silk tie. It took him ten minutes to get the tie right, and then the knot was a little lopsided. The clock in the hallway struck seven. The tie would have to do. He wanted to be at the ballet early enough to watch for Janet.

The thought of her made him whistle. Taking his brush and whistling a good Hank Williams tune, he tried to tame his hair into submission. It was hopeless. His hair always looked as if he'd just stepped off a Ferris wheel at the amusement park. Maybe it would be too dark for Doc to notice.

Still whistling, he got into his pickup truck and drove across town to the Civic Auditorium. He parked between a silver Cadillac and a black Mercedes, then strode down the sidewalk to the gaily lit auditorium.

Crowds of people milled around the foyer, some on the staircase, some just inside the glass double doors, chatting and laughing, their voices as discreet as the clothes they wore. Black satin, burgundy velvet and ivory silk. The women rustled when they moved. Charcoal gray and black pinstripes and pristine white. The men fairly squeaked when they moved, as if they had been too long in their three-piece business suits and needed oiling.

Smiling, Dan leaned against the stair railing and watched the front doors. "Nothing like being a canary at a convention of sparrows."

"I beg your pardon." A bejeweled matron passing by stopped to arch her painted-on eyebrows at him.

He smiled at her. "Lovely evening for the ballet, isn't it?"

"Yes. *Sleeping Beauty* is my favorite. Such drama, such magnificence, such..."

He didn't hear the rest of what she was saying, for at that moment Dr. Janet Hall walked through the front door. She was wearing a green velvet evening suit, stunning in its simplicity. Her rich hair was caught high on her head with a single diamond clasp. The real thing from the sparkle of it.

Never taking his gaze from Janet's face, he murmured an apology to the matron. "Excuse me, please. There's someone I have to see." *And touch.* Janet's soft rose-and-ivory skin beckoned to him across the crowded room. He started toward her, moving slowly down the stairs as if he were suddenly caught in a delicious wave of hot honey.

She became still, every muscle in her body tense and alert as she sensed herself being watched. Slowly she turned her head. One silky curl slipped its bond and curved softly against her cheek. She saw him, and her lips parted in surprise.

He was moving toward her with determination, his wild dark hair curling around his noble head, his old-fashioned

suit somehow looking elegant and just right on his big
frame. Even his pink shirt and red striped tie were exactly
right for him. There was nothing conservative and go-by-
the-book about Dan Albany. He was as bold and brash and
virile as a Thoroughbred at stud.

When he was so close she could see the tiny silver star-
bursts in the center of his Venetian-blue-glass eyes, he spoke.
"Hello, Doc. Fancy meeting you here."

Her indrawn breath escaped in a small hissing sound, and
her pulse fluttered in her throat like a trapped humming-
bird.

"Are you meeting someone?"

"No, I . . ."

"Good." Dan reached up and touched the soft curl on her
cheek. "Do you always look so delicious at the ballet?"

"Yes . . . No—I mean . . ."

Smiling, he took her arm and escorted her up the stairs.
"I'll have to make it a point to come more often."

"Let go of my arm. What are you doing here?"

Keeping a hold on her with one hand and taking a couple
of programs with the other, he led her into the auditorium.
"Which do you want me to do first? Let go, or tell you why
I'm here."

The fact was, she didn't want him to let go at all. And she
was foolishly giddy over his being at the ballet. Of course,
she knew what his game was. He was as transparent as
plastic sandwich bags. Love of music hadn't brought him
out this evening. He was out to prove his suitability.

Suddenly she smiled. Maybe she could turn the evening
to her advantage.

She squeezed the hand that was holding her arm and gave
him a coy smile. "I don't know why I'm being so testy. All
that fresh air this afternoon must have gone to my brain."

He could barely keep from laughing. Doc was flirting again. She'd affected such a syrupy drawl he'd half expected her to say "mah little ole brain." She even batted her eyelashes a time or two.

"I found the fresh air invigorating, myself. We'll have to do it again sometime."

Her cheeks got a shade pinker. He chuckled. "Play soccer, I mean."

"Of course. I knew what you meant." She detached herself from him and nodded toward the center section. "Are these seats all right with you?"

"They are perfect for what I have in mind."

Her pulse quickened as she took her seat. By now she didn't try to rationalize that phenomenon. Dan Albany was the cause, plain and simple. Fortunately she knew that an overactive pulse wasn't fatal.

"Mind your manners, Coach. You're at the ballet."

He slid into the seat beside her, stretching his long legs so that his right one was leaning against her thigh.

He winked at her. "I know. And I can't wait until they dim the lights."

"You're looking forward to the music, are you?"

"No. I'm looking forward to the dark. I have a few ideas about what a man and a woman should be doing when the lights go down and the music starts up."

"Like what, Coach? Eat hot dogs and raise their cholesterol levels?"

"A few delicacies, savored slowly, go well with a little night music."

"It's all a matter of taste, I suppose."

His smile lit the center of his eyes. The house lights dimmed, and he reached for her hand. "Taste...and touch," he whispered.

Janet was glad for the darkness. Dan's suggestive conversation had put her body in such a turmoil that she was sure it must be showing on her face. He was a wicked rogue, all right. Wicked and arrogant and unsuitable and charming. It was his charm that made her leave her hand in his. That and the compelling warmth of him.

She settled back in her comfortable chair and prepared to enjoy the ballet. *Sleeping Beauty* would be a feast for the senses, with magnificent backdrops, sparkling costumes, graceful dancing and music that stirred the soul. Tchaikovsky had always been a favorite composer of hers. The grandeur of his music was magic that transported her into another world.

But tonight he had some fierce competition. Dan was working a magic all his own, his strong fingers massaging her palm, making quick feather-light circles that were faintly erotic and highly disturbing.

He leaned over and whispered in her ear. "I never did trust a man who wore pink silk britches."

She stifled a giggle. It was amazing, this ability of his to make her forget decorum. Meaning to chastize him, she turned and found herself a whisper away from his mouth.

"Yes?" His breath fanned warmly across her cheeks.

Unconsciously the tip of her tongue circled her lips. "The music has started."

"So it has." In the dark his vivid blue eyes absorbed the light from the stage and mesmerized her. She might have gazed into them the rest of the evening, letting Sleeping Beauty fend for herself if Dan hadn't finally turned away. She felt as if she'd been released from a steam bath.

The music swept around her and through her. Tchaikovsky and Dan. It was a heady combination.

She sneaked a glance at him. He seemed as relaxed and comfortable as if he were enjoying a Southeastern Conference play-off baseball game on TV. His ability to adapt himself to any circumstance was uncanny. She'd wager a month's salary that he had never been to the ballet, but she couldn't tell it by looking at him now.

Suddenly he turned and caught her watching him. He winked and whispered to her behind his program, "It's amazing what a mighty sword can do for a man. I think she's going to go for that fop."

Trust him to find the humor in Sleeping Beauty's dramatic rescue.

"He's a prince."

"If I had a mighty sword would I be a prince?"

Her gaze raked across his broad chest and downward to his muscular legs. Even the suit couldn't disguise his obvious physical charms.

"You don't need a sword." The words were out before she realized what she was saying. To make matters worse, she was leaning so close in order not to disturb the people around her that her mouth was practically on Dan's ear. A slight movement of his head, and she found herself nose-to-nose with him.

"Thanks, Doc."

Before she could take back the compliment, he kissed her. The touch was feather-light and so brief it probably went unnoticed by the ballet fans, but it was a kiss nonetheless. She hastily sat back in her seat and fanned herself with her program. She had never carried on so at the ballet. And she'd never had as much fun.

Dan smiled to himself. He had expected to suffer through the ballet for the sake of proving his point, but instead he was actually enjoying himself. The music wasn't half bad, though he did prefer songs with words. He liked to hum along, and he liked to know what a man had on his mind when he wrote a particular piece of music. Still, there was something grand about Tchaikovsky's music. He even admired the dancers. It took superb physical fitness and not a little athletic prowess to do all that leaping and spinning. He could have done without the tight silk britches, though. He thought the male dancers looked silly.

Of course, being with Doc made all the difference in the world. He could have enjoyed a tooth-pulling exhibition with her. He guessed it was all that fire and passion she tried to keep under wraps that had him so intrigued.

He looked at her as the curtain rang down for intermission. She was still facing the stage, appearing as cool and unapproachable as ever.

He took up the challenge.

"Tell me, Doc..." She turned toward him. "Are you wearing black lace under that elegant suit?"

Her eyes widened, and it took her a minute to recover. Then, smiling, she leaned intimately close to him and murmured, "Is that a pass, Coach?"

It was his turn to be taken aback. He'd come to the ballet to take charge, not to be taken charge of. If she kept saying things like that he'd have her in his brass bed before the evening was over, and the devil take old-fashioned dream women.

Under the guise of relaxing, he leaned back in his chair far enough so that he wasn't completely intoxicated by the sight of that delicate rose skin and the scent of jasmine in her hair.

"No. It was just curiosity."

"Professional or personal?"

"Merely professional. You see, I'm doing this study of doctors with burgundy-wine hair and copper-penny eyes and rose-kissed skin."

"Any results, yet?"

"So far I've learned that they can't play soccer worth a hoot... but they're sexy as all get-out on a soccer field."

"Why, thank you, Coach."

"Nothing personal, you understand."

"Naturally. Anything else?"

"They claim to enjoy men cavorting in silk britches, but that doesn't keep them from lusting after coaches in out-of-style wool suits."

"Lusting!"

Three people standing in the aisle chatting turned their heads to grin at Dan and Janet. Her cheeks got hot, and she felt the urge to crown him with her program. Such undisciplined urges were entirely new to her. Dan was more dangerous than she had first thought. She'd have to tread carefully.

His eyes twinkling, he leaned over and whispered. "Do you think they'll spread the word?"

"It's hardly likely. I can't imagine who in Tupelo would be interested in our private affairs."

"Affair? I like your choice of words, Doc."

"Do you always do this?"

"What?"

"Put one and one together and get six?"

"I'd rather get eight."

"Eight?"

"Two parents, six kids. I plan to have a large family."

"So you've said," Janet reminded him. "But the size of your family is hardly any concern of mine."

"Since I'm so unsuitable?"

"Precisely."

"Ahh, Doc." He surprised her by leaning back in his seat and chuckling. Then he quirked one eyebrow at her and drawled, "How can you resist all this class and culture? Tchaikovsky, striped tie and red socks. What more can a woman want?"

"Red socks?"

"I thought they matched rather well." He lifted one pant leg to reveal the bright red socks.

She had to laugh. Not at him, but with him. As the house lights were dimming, they sat back in their seats and chuckled.

Dan Albany had his moments. She'd have to keep her guard up.

Janet Hall kept surprising him. He'd have to plan a tight defense.

As the prima ballerina came onto the stage, Janet sat back to enjoy the ballet. Thank goodness, Dan was behaving himself. He was leaning back in his own seat, watching the stage as if he really planned to pay attention to the dancers for a change.

Her relief was short-lived. Five minutes into the program she felt something fuzzy gliding up her leg. Not just fuzzy, hard and fuzzy. Electric currents pulsed through her as she realized what it was. She glanced down to confirm what she instinctively knew. In the semidarkness Dan's sock-clad foot was inching its sensuous way over her silk-stockinged calves.

The foot moved slowly, dragging back and forth, up and down until she felt her legs turn to butter. She stared straight ahead, pretending not to notice. Then the heat started. It crept its way up her legs, climbing higher and higher until it centered itself at the juncture of her thighs.

Passion had no common sense, at all, she decided. Nor was it subject to scientific analysis. It just seemed to happen, and no amount of rationale would make it go away.

Dan's toes were now drawing erotic circles behind her left knee. Except for the wicked smile on his face, he appeared to be watching the ballet with a single-minded fascination.

She leaned over and whispered, "Move your foot."

"Higher or lower?"

"Off."

"Ahh, Doc." He closed his eyes at the end of a long sigh. "There's no fun at all in that." His foot kept up its delicious massage.

Sleeping Beauty did a stunning jeté that wrung a collective gasp from the audience. Janet gasped, too. But not at the dancer. It was the lazy intimacy of Dan's massage that had her moaning.

The devilish gleam in his eyes was the only indication that he knew. He slid his arm nonchalantly across the back of her seat, letting it fall onto her shoulders. His index finger started a small, probing massage on her upper arm. Her velvet sleeve was no protection at all. Tongues of flame went licking across her chest.

Letting her neck go limp, she leaned back in her seat and closed her eyes.

Dan bent close and whispered, "Tired? I'll take you home to bed."

"Bed?" Her eyes flew open as she mouthed the word. Seeing his wicked grin, she closed them again and added, "The entertainment's not over yet."

"It certainly isn't." His fingers slid to the underside of her arm and began to caress the side of her breast. Her velvet suit heightened the sensuality of the touch.

She didn't know what Sleeping Beauty was doing now, nor did she care. She kept her eyes closed and her head back as if she'd been overcome by the music or was resting from a long and exhausting day at the clinic. If anybody noticed her, she hoped that's what they would think.

And Dan kept up his secret massages. By the time the ballet was over she was in such a heated, languorous state that she didn't want to move.

The house lights came up, and she heard Dan shuffling his feet around, trying to find his shoes.

"Lose something?" She opened her eyes and grinned at him.

"On the contrary. I think I found something."

"Dare I ask what?"

Under the guise of reaching into her lap for her program, he put his hand on her thigh and said softly, "I found one warm and willing lady doctor."

She had to take a deep breath before she could reply. "I'm amazed that a man accustomed to game tactics doesn't know one when he sees it."

"All that response was game tactics?"

"Of course." It was only the second inning and he was already winning the game. She had to do something to wipe that triumphant, knowing grin off his face. She put her hand on his upper arm in feigned sympathy. "Oh, Dan. My dear. Did you think I found you irresistible?"

His amused chuckle told her that never was a man in less need of sympathy than Dan Albany. He winked at her. "Most women do, Doc."

"As you've already discovered, I'm not 'most women.'"

"No. Just all woman." He stood up and smoothly took her elbow. "Allow me."

"I brought my own car."

"It's parked two rows back, is it? Waiting for you?"

Her only reply was a dignified lifting of her chin as she began to walk up the aisle. Dignity quickly went flying out the door. In the press of the crowd she was forced into full body contact with Dan. He took immediate advantage by sliding one arm discreetly down her hips and pulling her backward so that she was intimately aware of every stunning inch of him. His strong thighs brushed against the back of her legs and his broad chest fairly enveloped her back.

Her breathing became short. It was merely physical, she told herself. The overreaction of an uptight, too busy physician who had been without male companionship for longer than she cared to remember.

She was relieved when they reached the double doors at the back of the auditorium. Every time she was around this man she lost control. At their next skirmish she would definitely be in charge.

Already laying her battle plans, she turned to him. "Goodbye, Dan. It was lovely seeing you at the ballet."

Chuckling, he took her arm and escorted her down the steps. "Where is your car parked?"

"Thank you, but I don't need an escort to my car."

Paying her no mind, he guided her through the doors and toward the parking lot. "I won't have any trouble finding it. That Porsche can't be too hard to spot."

"Is this male-dominance obsession of yours typical of all coaches, or is it merely a personal quirk?"

"As you've probably discovered, I'm not 'all coaches.'"

"Touché. I'll concede the victory." She pointed into the darkness in the general direction of west. "I think my car's over there."

"You think! Dr. Hall, have you any idea what can happen to women alone in the dark?"

"Are you planning another demonstration?"

"Now that's an idea worthy of consideration." Dan stopped in a deserted corner of the parking lot between a sleek red Corvette and a metallic-blue Firebird. Putting one finger under Janet's chin, he lifted her face to his. Her quick intake of breath pleased him. It seemed the doctor wasn't immune to coaches after all.

The moonlight was reflected in her diamond hair clasp and shot silvery shafts across her skin. He felt an intense urge to kiss her, but he didn't want to carry his charade that far. She might get the idea that he was actually falling for her. And of course he was not.

But he was softening a little. That skin! He skimmed his index finger across her cheek.

She held her breath. What was happening to her control lately? she wondered. Maybe she needed a vacation. One as far away from Tupelo and Dan Albany as possible.

She steeled herself against his touch and looked straight into his eyes. "Shall I pucker up, Coach?"

His smile crinkled his eyes at the corners. "Not yet, Doc. I'm saving the big guns for later."

"I suppose you're waiting for me to ask what the big guns are?"

"No. I plan to surprise you."

"You know what they say about surprises, Coach?"

"Tell me, Doc. What do they say?"

"Surprises can sometimes backfire."

"That will never happen to me."

"You're immune to the caprices of life?"

"No. But I'm always prepared."

Janet laughed. She was going to have the time of her life proving just how unprepared he was.

"Well, Coach, since it seems that you're going to deprive me of a good-night kiss, why don't you escort me to my car? I need to go home to bed."

"Is that an invitation, Doc?" He walked her to the Porsche and leaned down to open the car door.

She slid into the driver's seat and put the key into the ignition. The engine hummed to life. Smiling up at him, she fired one last shot.

"Do you need one, Coach?"

She pulled her door shut before he had time to reply. It was a grand exit, worthy of generals, kings, queens and movie idols. She started chuckling as she backed out of the parking space. Dan might have won the skirmish in the auditorium, but she had vanquished him in the parking lot.

As she eased her car out of the lot, she spared one last glance at Dan in the rearview mirror. He was standing with his feet planted wide and his head thrown back, laughing. He didn't look like a defeated man. On the contrary, he looked like a man who had just begun to do battle.

She tapped her fingernails on the steering wheel and started whistling. Land, she hadn't whistled since she was twelve years old. It felt good.

The light on Gloster Street was red. While she was waiting for it to change, Janet glanced out her window and announced to the city at large, "It seems to me that what men and women do best in the dark is have fun."

The light changed and she headed north toward home, still whistling.

Chapter Five

Dan always enjoyed Sundays. There was something wonderfully uplifting about the faces of a churchgoing crowd. From his vantage point in the choir loft, he looked out over the audience. The sanctuary was nearly full. He grinned at his sister and her family. They took up an entire pew—Betty June, her husband Ron, seven-year-old Peter, six-year-old Merry and the three-year-old twins, Butch and Samuel. And Betty June was pregnant again. She'd always said she planned to have her own basketball team, and it looked as if she was well on her way.

He gave her a big wink, then turned his attention back to the service. The organ music started, and the choir director took up his baton. "Amazing Grace." It was his favorite song. And he sang louder than anybody, exuberantly off-key. Sometimes he hit a note and sometimes he didn't. But nobody seemed to mind. He was grateful to be in a group of people who loved him just the way he was.

Right in the middle of "how sweet the sound" he began to ponder the concept of love. The love of friends. That was easy to figure out. Friends seemed always to be around when you needed them, much like candy bars when you were hungry for chocolate. Romantic love. Now that was a different thing. He supposed it was anyway. He didn't have any experience. At least not yet.

Janet popped into his mind. He could see her as clearly as if she were sitting on the front pew, exactly the way she had looked last night, her hair pulled back, her skin glowing, her face rapt as she listened to the music. What was she doing right this minute? Was she in church somewhere singing this very same song? Or did she sing at all? He hoped so. Even if she didn't sing, he hoped she hummed. There was something about a woman who hummed that simply got next to a man. Not that he wanted her to get next to him. Except temporarily, of course. Long enough to prove his point.

Grinning broadly, he picked up the singing where he had left off. It was not until he'd completed a robust rendition of "When we've been there ten thousand years," that he realized everybody else was singing "Thro' many dangers, toils and snares."

Betty June lifted her eyebrows at him.

A few blocks away, Janet was having trouble following the sermon. Ordinarily she hung on every word Dr. Bascomb said. And if her attention wandered at all, it settled on her lovely and peaceful surroundings. There was no more beautiful sanctuary in town, she thought, than that of the church on Jefferson Street. Of course, that little touch of blue in the stained-glass window reminded her of Dan Albany's eyes. And she'd never before noticed Dr. Bascomb's hair. It was wild and untamed, different from Dan's only in color.

Where was he right now? she wondered. Was he in some great old church sitting in the front pew? She instinctively knew that he would never sit in the back. That wasn't his style.

Suddenly she felt a nudge on her shoulder.

Nellie Hodskins, who always sat on her right, leaned over and whispered to her, "Dr. Hall."

She jerked her attention back to the service. Good grief. Everybody in church was standing. Up front, Dr. Bascomb was just finishing the benediction. The service was practically over, and she'd hardly even noticed the beginning. Feeling a little chagrined, she stood up for the end. It was the least she could do.

Dan had barely shucked himself out of his sport coat and Sunday tie when he heard a clamor at his front door. From the volume of the racket it had to be either an invasion of Halloween trick-or-treaters lost since last October, or the arrival of Betty June and her brood.

It was Betty June. She came bustling through the door before Dan could get it completely open, talking every breath.

"You might as well not hem and haw around the bush. I saw the way you were acting at church today—Butch, get off that hall tree before you fall and kill yourself. Like somebody who had a seatful of firecrackers and didn't know where to find the water bucket—Merry, if you jerk on my skirt one more time you're going to pull it plumb in two." She swept through his hallway like the leader of a parade, trailing husband and children and mixing metaphors for all she was worth.

Dan plucked Butch off the hall tree, swung him onto his shoulders for a piggyback ride and took little Samuel by the hand. "It's 'beat around the bush,' Betty June."

The correction was lost on her; she had already gone on to bigger and better things. "Ron, honey, would you get me a glass of water? Thank you, sweetheart." She settled into the rocking chair right on top of Janet Hall's green silk scarf. "I declare, a woman in my condition feels just like a rolling stone that grass won't grow under—Peter, if you turn that bookcase over on yourself, I won't be responsible. I declare—" She stopped talking suddenly, noticing the green silk scarf that was trailing down the side of the chair. Lifting one hip, she pulled it out and rubbed it between her fingers.

Even from his chair on the opposite side of the fireplace, Dan caught a lingering whiff of jasmine.

"Dan, when did you start wearing silk scarves and perfume?"

He chuckled. "The scarf belongs to Janet Hall."

"*Dr.* Janet Hall?"

"Yes."

Smiling, Betty June folded the scarf neatly into a small square and laid it on the table beside her chair. "She's the best pediatrician in town. Beautiful, too. Well, my goodness..." She gave Dan a big grin. "I'm just as happy as a jaybird about all this."

"About what?"

"You know...you and Dr. Hall...I wonder if I'll still have to call her *Dr.* Hall."

Dan leaned back in his chair and laughed. Betty June could take six eggs and make an omelet big enough to feed everybody in town.

After his mirth had subsided he said, "Betty June, when we get ready for the wedding we'll let you plan it."

"Are you teasing me?"

"What do you think?"

"Oh dear, I guess I've jumped over the gun again."

"That's 'jumped the gun'—or 'jumped over the haystack.'"

"Why would anybody want to jump over a haystack?"

Ron came back with the glass of water in time to hear the last snatch of Betty June's sentence. "What's this about a haystack? Has one of our children set it on fire?"

"No. We're just discussing my brother and his new girlfriend—Dr. Hall."

"*Our* Dr. Hall?"

"One and the same."

"Well, congratulations, old man." Ron sat down beside the fireplace, stretched out his long legs and began to rock. "There's nothing like a good woman to keep a man happy. I should know."

"Congratulations are premature. The only thing Dr. Hall and I have in common is a big stray dog."

Betty June nodded and smiled in a maternal sort of way. "Ron, honey, why don't you run downtown and get us a couple of large pizzas for lunch? And do you mind taking the kids? Dan and I have things to do."

After Ron and the children had gone, Dan turned to his sister. "What was that all about?"

"Can I help it if I want to be alone with my brother once in a while?"

"As you so often say, I smell a skunk in Denmark."

Betty June stood up and smoothed her skirt over her voluminous stomach. "Put a good, slow dance tune in the tape deck, Dan. I'm going to give you a dance lesson."

"You know I despise dancing."

"Nevertheless, you're going to learn how. You never know when you might get the urge to ask a certain beautiful lady doctor out dancing."

Dan laughed. "Mama didn't teach any of us subtlety, did she?"

He selected a tape of haunting Gershwin tunes; then, with all the enthusiasm of a man being led to his execution, he held out his arms to his sister.

Janet had planned to spend her Sunday afternoon doing something she really enjoyed. There were several current fiction bestsellers she hadn't yet had time to read. And there was a Sunday afternoon concert by the high-school chamber choir that would be wonderful. Then there was an excellent documentary on ETV—"DNA: Changing Life's Genetic Blueprint."

She didn't know what possessed her to be on her knees in the middle of her kitchen floor scrambling through ancient cookbooks for a peanut butter cookie recipe. She rationalized her behavior by telling herself that she would invite Mr. Jed over for home-baked cookies. Then in order to make her rationale work, she had to get up off the floor and call him to come over.

She did, and within fifteen minutes he was seated in one of her kitchen chairs watching her assemble the ingredients for cookies.

"This is a pleasant surprise. I didn't know you could bake cookies, Janet."

"This is a first for me," she admitted, starting to measure the flour. "An experiment, so to speak."

"I hope I come out better than some of those laboratory rats the doctors use."

Janet chuckled. "You don't have to worry about a thing. The worst that can happen is that you'll get a case of indigestion." She cracked eggs, measured sugar and greased the cookie tin with a vengeance. Making cookies was going to be a breeze. She'd show that Dan Albany. Any old body could make cookies.

While she and Mr. Jed talked, she got her first batch made and into the oven. When the buzzer went off fifteen minutes later, she took the cookies out. They were golden brown, perfectly round, perfectly beautiful cookies. She was proud of herself.

She got two plates and two glasses of milk. "Nothing like home-baked cookies and a big glass of milk for a Sunday afternoon snack," she chattered as Mr. Jed bit into one. "Eat up, Mr. Jed. There are plenty more where that one came from."

"I sincerely hope not."

Janet knew that old folks usually said exactly what they meant, but that was a little blunt, even coming from Mr. Jed. She took a bite of her own cookie and promptly had a choking fit. When she had herself back under control, she stood up, whisked their plates away and dumped the cookies into the garbage can.

"I obviously omitted a vital ingredient. But one setback does not constitute failure. Right, Mr. Jed?" She grinned at her old friend.

"I'm having the time of my life, Janet. I'll stay here and be your guinea pig as long as you want to bake."

The second batch stuck to the cookie tin and came out in crumbs hardly big enough for the birds, and the third batch came out black as a pair of tuxedo pants and just about as tasty.

Mr. Jed studied Janet with his keen old eyes as she started mixing the fourth batch.

"I've never seen you this fired up about domestic chores. Any particular reason?"

Flour drifted to the floor as Janet turned to face him. "There's a man who thinks I'm not his type, and I'm bound and determined to prove him wrong."

"The proof is in the baking, is it?"

Janet thought about that for a while; then she raked the raw cookie dough off her fingers and crossed toward the kitchen sink to wash her hands. Of course the proof was not in the baking. All the things Dan thought he wanted in a woman were superficial. One could buy perfectly delicious cookies at any bakery. And hand-knit sweaters could be purchased by the dozen from flea markets and craft shops. What made a woman the right type for a particular man was something much more subtle, much less easily defined. For want of a better word, she called it sparks.

Smiling, she turned to Mr. Jed. "How did you know?"

"It's the wisdom of old age, child."

"I think I just have time to run down to Kroger's deli for cookies before I have to leave for hospital rounds."

"I'll be waiting right here."

By the time Janet had changed her clothes, gotten the cookies, shared a small snack with Mr. Jed and finished her hospital rounds, the sun had faded from the sky and a light drizzle was falling. She glanced at her watch. It was still early, and if she hurried she might catch the veterinary clinic open.

Ducking her head against the drizzle, she dashed for her car.

It was raining in earnest by the time Janet arrived at the clinic. Through the haze of rain she could see several vehicles. That meant the clinic was open.

She parked her Porsche as close to the door as she could and stepped out into the rain. If she had paid more attention to the weather report and less to burning cookies, she might have known to wear a raincoat and carry an umbrella, and she certainly would have known better than to dress in her red-wool Halston suit.

She made a quick dash for the front door and ran solidly into a very large man.

"Excuse me." She looked up into the laughing blue eyes of Dan Albany.

"As I live and breathe. If it's not the good Dr. Hall." He brushed rain off her suit and tucked a wet curl behind her ear. "How are you, Doc?"

"Wet. Do we have to stand out here in the rain talking?"

"I play better on a wet field." He brushed the back of his hand lightly across her damp cheek.

Shivers climbed up her spine. "Are you aiming for a goal, or is this merely a pass?"

"That depends on the receiver." His hand slid under her chin and tipped her face upward toward his.

The shivers that had been slithering over her spine now walked on little cat feet over her chest. Her breathing became restricted. She glanced around, half hoping for a timely interruption, but they were the only two people crazy enough to stand in the rain outside the clinic door.

She swung her gaze back to Dan's face. It was tight with controlled passion. Her heart climbed high in response, and it took all her effort to keep her reply light.

"Don't underestimate your receiver, Coach. I can handle anything you can toss my way."

"Then shall we try for a small pass?"

Cupping her face lightly between his palms, Dan bent down and kissed her. Her lips were cold and wet with rain. Dan tasted, teased, licked away the dampness. He had meant the kiss to be a small play, a diversionary tactic to throw her off guard. But his heart got in on the act. A shining started deep in his soul. His heart lifted high as if it had eagle wings and soared into a brightness almost beyond bearing. And suddenly the small tasting was not enough.

He slid his hands down her shoulders and around to the small of her back. Pulling her closer, he deepened the kiss. Janet felt of damp wool and female softness. She smelled of rain and jasmine and faintly of hospital disinfectants, as if her profession were some inborn part of her.

She's not for you, Coach, Dan's inner voice of reason told him. But he ignored it. At least for the moment.

He held onto her, absorbing the richness of her kiss, until some small part of him made him let go. Feeling warm inside and slightly shaken by her easy ability to turn him away from his purpose, he released her and stepped back.

Except for the high color in her cheeks, she still looked every inch the unflappable doctor, wet Halston suit and all.

Janet ran her hand lightly over her face to brush away any lingering drops of rain, but mainly to give herself time to collect herself.

"Well, Coach. Since the game is over, I suggest we go inside to see our dog."

"The game isn't over, Doc. It's merely intermission time." He held open the clinic door. "After you."

"What's this? A sudden attack of manners?"

"I get these attacks every now and then." Grinning, he leaned down to whisper in her ear. "A few more kisses like that, Doc, and I'll forget my manners entirely."

"I'm equal to the occasion."

Dan stepped back and let his wicked gaze sweep over her. Wet red wool became her. "I do believe you are, Doc," he said softly.

Janet was saved by the arrival of Billie Jean Haskins. Having fully recovered from her blunders on their previous visit, she approached them with all the vigor and enthusiasm of an army sergeant facing a roomful of new recruits.

"Well, I declare. Dr. Hall. Don't you look as pretty as a picture." She glanced at Dan. "And Mr. Albany. My, my,

I'm glad to see the two of you here together. I guess that means you made up.''

"Made up?'' Janet had a sudden vision of romantic little Billie Jean Haskins peeking out the window while she and Dan had been kissing on the doorstep. She could see her reputation as a cool and sophisticated woman doctor disappearing before her very eyes.

And Dan made matters worse. He stepped close and put his arm around her shoulders.

"We certainly did, honey. I said to myself, now is that any way to treat a beautiful lady doctor?'' He winked and squeezed her shoulders. "Besides, making up is always the best part of any relationship.''

Billie Jean beamed. "Oh, I think so, too. Why, sometimes I deliberately pick a fight with Wayne Earl—that's my boyfriend, drives a truck for Viking—just so we can kiss and make up. My, my. How nice.'' She flipped the book she was carrying until she found the name of their dog. "I guess you two came to see Harvey. Follow me.''

As they fell into step, Janet looked at Dan across the top of Billie Jean's head. "What relationship?'' she mouthed.

"Opponents.''

Billie Jean jerked her head around. "Did you say something, Mr. Albany?''

"I said, it's almost upon us, this visit with our dog.''

She beamed at him again, obviously content that she had handled her job to perfection this time. No blunders and no attacks of acute embarrassment. "It sure is.'' She pushed open a door and swept through. "You two wait right here. I'll get Harvey for you.''

They waited on straight-backed chairs until she came back, carrying Harvey as carefully as if he were an armful of fragile glass. "Here he is. All set to see his mommy and daddy.'' Billie Jean placed Harvey carefully on the examining table and left the two of them alone with him.

Harvey's tail thumped the table and he whined.

Janet felt a lump in her throat as she rose from her chair. But she had been carefully schooled to keep her emotions in check around sick patients. By the time she reached Harvey, she was fully in control. She stroked his fur and petted his head. ''How are you, old boy? Feeling better?''

Dan didn't try to hold back his emotions. He leaned down and nuzzled his head against the big dog's head. ''Harvey, do you have any idea how much I've missed you? You old cuddlebum, you've had me worried half to death.'' He took the dog's face between his hands and bent toward him, nose-to-nose. ''You've got to get well so I can get you out of here, boy. Do you know how many hot dogs I've had to throw away since you've been gone? And there's not a soul around to eat the steak bones.''

Janet was touched. Dan's eyes had the suspicious gleam of tears, and his voice was gruff with emotion. She envied him. Just this afternoon on her hospital rounds she had felt like leaning her head on little Randy Sanderford's pillow and crying. She had stopped his seizures, but his tests didn't look good. Not good at all.

She cleared her throat and stepped back from the table. She felt as if one tear, one word too sympathetically spoken, would release a flood of emotion that she might never dam up again.

''He looks good, Dan. I think he's going to be fine.''

Dan turned and studied her with his piercing blue eyes.

''Is that your professional opinion?''

The way he said it, clipped and cool, made the question sound like an accusation.

''That's what I am, Dan. A doctor.''

''Is it also who you are, Janet?''

He usually called her Doc. And he was usually either playful or teasing or passionate. Now he was deadly serious. The humor was gone from his face and his eyes were the cold blue of winter lakes in an ice storm.

A whirlwind of emotions swept through her, and she swayed. Dan started toward her, but she held up her hand to stop him.

"Don't—"

"Janet . . ." He took another step toward her.

"Fatigue. It goes with my profession."

He reached out a hand, and his touch was tender on her cheek. Suddenly it was too much—Harvey, and Randy in the hospital, and Dan turning her inside out and upside down.

She drew back, and he let his hand fall to his side.

"You can tell Harvey goodbye for me."

She left quickly, her high heels making sharp staccato sounds on the tile floor. But she left with dignity, her chin held high and her back held straight. Dignity and control. They had been her hallmark and her habit for many years. And they wouldn't let her down now.

She got through the reception room and into her car before the first shudder passed through her. Clenching her hands into fists so tight her fingernails bit into her palms, she leaned her head against the steering wheel.

"I won't cry. I can't afford to cry." She took a minute longer to pull herself together, then she lifted her head, put her key into the ignition and drove home.

The quiet beauty of her apartment welcomed her, but for once it didn't provide solace. Standing in the middle of her living room, dripping water on her expensive rug, she began to unbutton her jacket. Her fingers trembled.

"Dan Albany," she whispered. "What have you done to me?"

* * *

Dan felt lower than a worm. He stood, watching Janet walk out the door, and for the first time in his life he was completely flabbergasted. What had he said? What had he done?

When the door closed behind her, he walked back to the table and patted the big dog's head. "My God, Harvey. I can't believe I said that. Did you see the look on her face? She looked like a lovely porcelain figurine that had just been shattered. What has happened to me?" He cuddled the dog some more, taking comfort from the thumping tail and the soft whines. "I thought I was some hotshot Romeo. Heck, I used to think I knew more about making women happy than any man in the world. Some expert I turned out to be."

Dan stared into space for a while and tried to think what to do. Women problems. They were entirely new to him.

He gave Harvey's head an absentminded pat. "Do you mind if I cut this visit short, old boy? I have some tall apologizing to do."

He left Harvey with Billie Jean Haskins and drove across town to Janet's condo. The lights were on inside her apartment. He sat in his pickup for a while, taking comfort from the thought of her inside a warm and cozy room. He drummed his fingers on the steering wheel and whistled a tuneless song. Now that he was here, what in the world was he going to say? He felt like a fool. Was he really the same man who had only recently bragged about the joys of making up? "Get moving, Coach," he said aloud. "Are you a man or a wimp?" Still whistling nervously between his teeth, he got out of his truck and climbed the steps to her condo. He punched the dinky little buzzer, and then in a fever of impatience he lifted his hand and banged loudly on the door.

The door swung open and he saw Janet. She was wearing a soft-looking pink robe belted at the waist and her hair was wrapped in a pink towel. Backlit by the glow of her lamps, she looked like a pink-sugar angel come to life. He stood in the rain, staring.

"Won't you come in?"

Her voice was cool and formal, like a schoolteacher talking down to an unruly child. And he felt as tongue-tied as a disobedient student.

He stepped inside and was immediately struck by the differences between his home and hers. Her apartment was elegant, immaculate and expensive. He couldn't afford Waterford crystal, but he knew it when he saw it. Careful not to knock the ornate bowl of silk flowers off its mahogany perch, he stepped into her hallway.

"I suppose you came to tell me about Harvey," she said over her shoulder as she led the way into her sitting room.

Everything was the color of pale sherbet. He felt big and awkward.

"Well, actually, no." He cleared his throat and looked around for a chair that might be big enough to support his weight.

Janet was amused by his obvious discomfort. Amused and touched. Standing there dripping on her white rug, his wet curly hair plastered beguilingly to his head, his face a study in wicked innocence, Dan Albany tugged at her heartstrings. She decided to put him out of his misery.

"Why don't you take that big rocker by the fireplace? Don't worry; it's sturdy enough to hold an elephant."

"I'm hardly an elephant." Laughing, he eased himself into the chair. "But I am a jackass."

"Always?" She smiled as she sat on the sofa and tucked her legs under her.

"Not always. Only when I'm confronted by gorgeous lady doctors in wet, red designer suits."

"I see."

"Do you?"

Her smile got bigger. "I believe that I'm hearing an apology."

"You are." He stretched his long legs toward the cold fireplace, made a careful tent of his fingers and propped them under his chin. He gazed at her thoughtfully for a while. It was a comfortable silence. Neither of them felt the need to fill it with words.

Finally Dan spoke. "I'm not good at this, you know."

"That makes it all the more charming."

"Charming?"

"Sometimes."

He smiled at her. "I'd be willing to make a jackass of myself again to hear you tell me that."

"Surely other women have called you charming."

"No one who counts."

Across the room his blue gaze burned into her, and the silence stretched between them again. But this time there was a tension in the stillness, a breathless waiting, as if some long-anticipated event were about to take place.

Janet felt a pleasant heat seep into her bones. She leaned her head against the back of the sofa, never taking her eyes off Dan's.

"I truly am sorry, Janet." His voice was as soft and rich as a blues song, and just as mesmerizing. She let the melody wash over her. "I had no right to judge you or your profession. Each person feels pain and joy and . . . love differently."

She noticed his slight hesitation on the word "love." For some reason, it gave her pleasure.

"Thank you, Dan."

"This is getting easier all the time. You accept apologies very graciously."

She gave him a wicked grin. "Would you like to make up now?"

"I'm not sure I can be trusted."

She chuckled. "Over a plate of cookies."

"Ahh, Doc. How you disappoint me!" His exuberant, teasing good humor returned. "Cookies are second best, but they will be an acceptable substitute."

"Good. You wait right there."

When she got up from the couch her robe gaped open, and he caught an enticing glimpse of long, elegant legs.

She saw him watching her. With languid movements she pulled her robe shut, belting it tighter around the waist, her gaze never leaving his. A vibrant silence sang around the room. His eyes darkened, and she wet her dry lips with her tongue. He half rose from his chair, and her heart thumped hard against her ribs.

Suddenly he sank back into his chair. "About those cookies..."

"They're chocolate-chip."

"One of my favorites."

"I'll be right back." Janet escaped to the kitchen and leaned against the counter until she could regulate her heartbeat. Dan wasn't just a man sitting in her apartment: he was a presence that filled it. His big voice and his big laughter and his big body seemed to dwarf her fragile chairs and crystal accessories. A woman could get used to having a man like that around, a big, vibrant man who wore life like a charm around his neck.

She left her resting place at the kitchen counter and took the bag of cookies out of the pantry. Just like home-baked. That's what Mr. Jed had said about them.

Suddenly she smiled. Why not? She arranged the cookies on a platter and threw the bag into the garbage can. Then she poured two big glasses of milk and went back into the sitting room.

"Here you are, Dan. Freshly baked today."

"You baked cookies?"

"Yes. This afternoon." Her conscience twinged only a little bit. She *had* baked cookies. Four batches. All of them unspeakably bad. But Dan didn't have to know that. She was out to teach him a lesson.

He took a handful and settled back in his chair with his glass of milk.

"Hmm, these are delicious."

"I thought so, too." She sipped her milk and watched him over the rim of her glass.

"There's nothing like home-baked cookies on a winter's day to make a man feel good."

"You're very easy to please."

He ate two more cookies. "Not every woman can make cookies like this."

"I agree." Wholeheartedly. She was one of those women who couldn't. She suppressed her smile and egged him on. "I spent all afternoon baking."

He held up one perfect cookie. "Doc, these are worth an afternoon's work. Don't you agree?"

"Absolutely."

He took another bite. "Hmm. Pure gold. I'd give these cookies a blue ribbon."

She couldn't hold back her laughter any longer. It spilled out in a merry peal.

"I knew you'd be pleased with the compliment, but I didn't know you'd be that tickled."

She wiped tears of laughter from her eyes. "You should see your face."

"My face? What about my face?" Suspicious now, he set his glass of milk aside and stood up.

"You look so smug, and I-told-you-so."

"About what?"

"The cookies."

"Well, Doc. I think you did a great job baking them."

"I didn't bake them."

"You said you did."

"No. I said they were baked this afternoon and that I baked all afternoon."

The light was beginning to dawn. He sank back into his chair and looked at the cookie in his hand. "You didn't bake these?"

"No. These were made by the experts at Kroger's who make their living baking cookies for people like me who are both too busy and too inept to provide goodies for themselves."

"I see."

"Not yet, you don't." She got up off the sofa and took his hand. "Come with me."

In the kitchen she opened the pantry door and pulled out her garbage can. Then she whisked off the lid and pointed dramatically. "There. The results of my first and only attempt at home-baked cookies."

Dan eyed the pile of burned crusts and broken crumbs and soggy dough. As he gazed into the garbage can he had a sudden vision of Doc in the kitchen with flour on her nose, trying to make sense out of recipes and mixing bowls and baking pans. All that must have been as foreign to her as performing surgery would be to him. And yet she had tried. For him.

His heart jumped into his throat and his eyes misted over. "Doc, I am truly humbled."

She had meant to give him a pert reply until she saw his face. "Oh, Dan." She reached out and softly caressed his cheek. "I'm sure some dream women can bake cookies, but I can't."

He covered her hand with his. "Home-baked cookies don't seem to matter anymore."

They stood that way for a while. Finally Dan stirred. To-night Janet was too much temptation for him. Maybe she couldn't bake cookies, and maybe that was all right with him. But still she was a doctor and he was a coach. It was not a match made in heaven, and he'd do well to remember that. The knowledge made him extraordinarily blue.

He gave her a reckless grin, hoping it covered his true feelings. "Well, thanks for the cookies, Doc. And for the lesson."

"Any time, Coach."

She watched him leave the kitchen. His footsteps were loud on the tile floor, then muffled as he walked over her white rug. Finally she heard the front door close behind him.

"Any time," she whispered.

Chapter Six

Monday mornings were always a peak time at Janet's clinic. Mothers sometimes complained that there was a conspiracy among children to wait until Saturday night to get sick. That way the parents had most of the weekend to worry until they could get to the doctor's office bright and early Monday morning.

Most of her patients had the usual childhood complaints, upset stomachs, allergy rashes and winter colds. Still, it was a very long day at the clinic. And after that she had hospital rounds.

She saved Randy Sanderford for last. He was sitting up in the narrow hospital bed, surrounded by teddy bears, comic books and helium-filled balloons.

"Hey, Dr. Hall." He held up a comic book. "Look what I got."

The anti-seizure drug he was taking had made his entire body round and puffy, but his eyes were still bright in his pale face. Janet crossed the room and stood beside his bed.

"Another new comic book, Randy? Tell me about it."

"It's Batman. Gosh, he can do anything. And he has a neat car."

While he talked, she leaned closer and took his small hand, pressing her fingers into his pulse. It was still high and thready. She rubbed the small arm in compassion.

"That is a neat car, Randy."

"When I get big, I'm going to have me a Batmobile like that."

A lump came into Janet's throat. The tests hadn't been completed yet, but she suspected that Randy Sanderford would never "get big." Her heart cried for him.

She stepped back from the bed and assumed a professional manner. "I hope you will, Randy." She flipped open his chart and began to make rapid notations. "The nurses tell me you're being very good about eating all your food and taking all your medicine."

"I'm a little man. That's what Mommy calls me."

"Yes, you are. You're a fine little man." She closed his chart and moved toward the door. "Good night, Randy. I'll see you tomorrow."

"Good night, Dr. Hall. Don't let the bedbugs bite."

It was seven-thirty by the time she left the hospital—too late to visit Harvey. She drove home on Gloster Street, taking pleasure in the city lights that pierced the winter darkness. There was something comforting about beacons of light in darkness. She decided that as soon as she got home she would turn all the lamps down low and light a few candles.

As she parked her Porsche, she glanced toward Mr. Jed's door. He usually watched out his window for her to come home so he could stick his head out and greet her. Tonight she didn't see him. She'd better check.

She had to punch his buzzer three times before he answered the door. She was already having visions of getting the landlady and finding him inside suffering a heart attack.

When he finally came to the door, he was wearing rumpled striped pajamas and a big, self-satisfied grin. "Land sakes, Janet. What brings you over so late?"

"I got worried when I didn't see your smiling face."

"I've got a little secret." He glanced around to see if anybody was watching, and then he grabbed her wrist and pulled her inside. "If you promise not to tell, I'll show you."

"I promise. What in the world are you up to?"

He produced a weekly tabloid and flipped open to the Lonely Hearts section. Tapping his finger against one of the ads, he said, "Here. Read this."

"Handsome, spry senior citizen seeks mate," it said. "Looking for a woman who loves travel, opera, baseball, square dancing and laughter. Please reply quickly because I'm not getting any younger." The address followed.

"You, Mr. Jed?"

"Shoot, yes. Just because there's snow on the roof doesn't mean there's no fire in the oven. When I finally decided you were too young, I took action." He winked, then went to his rolltop desk and picked up a handful of letters. "Look here. I've already had six replies."

She was torn between laughter and sympathetic tears. Aloneness was fine, but loneliness was a terrible thing. "I hope this works out for you, Mr. Jed. But you know that you always have me."

"I know that, honey. But it's not the same as having a mate." He patted her hand. "You ought to take out one of these, Janet."

"I don't think so."

"Unless you've already found somebody." He eyed her keenly. "Didn't I see a big, handsome fellow on your doorstep last night?"

"Dan Albany."

"Is that the one you were baking cookies for?"

"Yes."

He chuckled and plucked a piece of paper off his desk. "I don't think we'll be needing this, after all."

"What is that?"

Grinning, he held it out to her. It was a typewritten ad, addressed to the Lonely Hearts column: "Young, beautiful female doctor looking for handsome companion. Must be intelligent, educated, industrious, but above all warm, fun-loving, tender and passionate. Please hurry."

Janet slowly lowered the paper. "You wouldn't have."

He chuckled. "I would. What are friends for if not to help each other?"

Laughing, she hugged him. "Mr. Jed, what am I going to do with you?"

He held two pictures out to her. "Help me choose between Glory Ethel and Magdaline Sue."

Both were gray-haired women who appeared to be in their early seventies. "They're both lovely," she said, and she meant it. "But Mr. Jed, don't you think you need to meet them and get to know them before you make a decision?"

"Oh, I'm planning on it." He tapped one of the pictures with his forefinger. "I'm kinda leaning toward Glory Ethel. But I guess I'll give it some more thought."

"You do that. Good night, Mr. Jed."

By the time she got to her own apartment it was eight-thirty. She pulled her coat off and hung it in the hall closet. Her hand brushed against something soft. Dan's sweatshirt. She rubbed the sleeve against her cheek. A faint masculine scent clung to the fabric.

On impulse she decided to return the shirt. Immediately. Why not? It was still early, and she had to get it back to him sometime.

At first she thought she'd call and tell him she was coming, and then she decided to surprise him. After all, hadn't he said he was always prepared for surprises?

Ten minutes later she was standing in front of Dan's double front doors, holding his sweatshirt and knocking. She could hear loud music coming from inside the house. That meant he was home. She knocked again, louder.

When there was still no response, she pressed closer to the beveled-glass ovals in his front door and peeked inside. The long expanse of hallway looked exactly as she remembered it—wooden floors gleaming softly with wax and old age; the hall tree, enduring nobly under its weight of letter jackets and baseball caps and umbrellas; Victorian sconces on the walls casting a soft glow on the elegant fading wallpaper.

She decided that Dan must have gone out and forgotten to turn off his stereo. She was just turning to leave when she caught a glimpse of someone coming slowly into the hallway. Not just someone. Dan. She leaned closer to get a better look. What she saw made her smile.

Big Coach Dan Albany, completely unaware that he had company, was waltzing stiffly into his hallway, hanging onto a mop. His lips were moving as if he were desperately counting the rhythm of each laborious footstep.

She watched a while longer in silent, secret pleasure; and then she knocked on his door again. Beside the hall tree, he missed a beat and turned his head toward the door. Janet knocked again. Still holding the mop, Dan walked to the door.

"Janet. My goodness. Come in. I didn't hear you knocking."

She stepped into the hallway and nodded toward his mop. "Doing a little housecleaning?"

"No. That's Betty June."

"Betty June?"

"Actually, it's Betty June's substitute. My sister's been trying to teach me to dance." He propped the mop against the wall. "Here. Let me take your coat."

He hung her coat on the hall tree and led her into his den. It was like walking into the arms of a good friend, she thought. Real logs in the fireplace glowed and snapped in welcome, and the light coming from the lamps was pink and softly diffused by the Victorian shades. Dan's idea of home decoration took on an entirely new meaning to Janet.

He turned the volume down on the stereo and the music became a lovely whispered melody that added to the grace and charm of the room. She stood beside the warm glow of the fire and felt some tightly controlled part of herself give in to the simple graciousness of his house.

From across the room he smiled at her. Such a wonderful smile. It turned her heart upside down.

"I'm glad to see you, Janet."

Memories of yesterday swept over her—the kiss in the rain, the way he had looked at her when he had come to apologize. The game they were playing with each other had subtly shifted in a way that she hadn't intended. Was he aware of the change, too? Or was this new intensity all a part of his game plan?

She was equal to the occasion. She had to be.

Smiling, she held out his sweatshirt. "I'm returning your property."

"That's a favorite old standby of mine." He crossed the room and reached for the shirt. Their hands touched. Maintaining the contact, he looked deep into her eyes. "If this shirt could talk, would it tell me how it felt to cover your body?''

She sucked her breath in sharply. "It kept me warm."

"Ahh, yes. Warmth. An essential element in any relationship, don't you agree?''

"It's certainly essential in the relationship between a woman and her coat."

"Or a woman and her man."

With the fire warming her legs and Dan's touch heating her heart, Janet felt she was slowly melting and blossoming, like an ice-encased daffodil that had waited too long for spring.

"Yes," she whispered. "According to experts, there is a certain warm regard between people who..."

"...fall in love?''

"Yes."

Without taking his eyes off her, he tossed his sweatshirt toward the rocker. Then he cupped her face. "Are we falling in love, Janet?''

She struggled for control. "I think two normal healthy adults, given the right circumstances and enough proximity, naturally react in certain ways."

"What ways?''

Her tongue flicked out over her lips. "With certain biological urges..."

"Like this?" He traced her cheeks, then moved his hands slowly down her throat. She felt the fabric of her blouse rustle as he undid the top two buttons. One hand slipped inside and rested on her chest. Her heart bounced against his palm.

"Yes."

"And this?" His index finger pushed inside her lacy bra and began to tease her nipple.

"Ahh, yes."

His free hand caught her hips and pulled them into his. His biological urges were stunningly apparent. Unable to prevent herself, she pressed closer.

He groaned and slammed his mouth down on hers. The kiss was a thunderous explosion, a reckless joining of two people whose needs could no longer be denied. Ancient, primitive forces controlled them.

One of Dan's hands slid into the heavy silk of her hair, and he gently twisted her head back to gain freer access to her mouth. She opened for him, welcoming his hot kisses and the heavy stroking of his tongue. Desire flamed hard and bright through her, and she clutched at his shoulders, desperate to have him closer, to be one with him, heart to heart, flesh against flesh, sating the raging appetites he had loosed in her. Her nails dug into his back.

Dan drank the heady sweetness of her mouth, inhaled the exotic fragrance of her hair, absorbed the rich female softness of her body. He wanted more. He wanted to be inside her, to find solace and comfort and release in her sweet, hot flesh.

Groaning, he began to rock his hips against hers. Where would it end? he wondered. Would their game end in one wild, wanton joining beside his fire? It was too soon. There were things yet that he wanted to prove to her. He had to... Oh, God. He had to taste more of her.

His mouth left hers and roamed down the side of her throat. Her head tilted back on a limp neck. He felt the heavy beat of her pulse against his lips, heard soft, murmuring pleasure sounds deep in her throat. He nudged aside her blouse and lowered his head to her breast. Her skin was soft and silky, rosy and glowing. He laved it with hot, wet strokes.

"Dan, please..."

He didn't know whether it was a plea to stop or an entreaty to continue. But the sound of her voice brought him back to his senses. Passion wasn't to be his proving ground.

He gentled her down with tender kisses on her breast, her throat, her lips. And at last he lifted his head. Her eyes were wide and bright, and her face was flushed. Without a word, he buttoned her blouse.

"I think you proved your point rather nicely." Her voice was shaky.

"You think we identified those biological urges?"

"Most of them."

He took a long, deep breath to get himself back under control. It helped, but not enough. Moving slightly away from her, he backed toward the fire pretending to warm himself.

Janet sank into the rocking chair beside the fire.

"Tired?"

"It's been a long day."

"The sweatshirt could have waited. You should be home resting."

His concern was genuine. She liked that about him. When Dan pretended, he told you so.

"I was restless. I felt the need to—" She stopped, not certain exactly what her needs were nor how she could explain that to Dan.

"To see me? I'm flattered."

She smiled. "You're arrogant."

"That, too."

They watched each other across the small space that separated them, both slightly shaken by their torrid kiss, both waiting for a cue, like actors on a stage who had suddenly discovered that the script had been changed. It was Dan who finally broke the silence.

"I'm glad you came over."

"So am I."

The fire crackled in the grate and the soft music swirled around them.

"Gershwin." This time it was Janet who spoke.

"What?" Dan seemed to come back from a distant place.

"The music. It's Gershwin, isn't it?"

"Yes. 'Someone to Watch over Me.' It's the song my sister selected for my dance lessons. I think she was trying to tell me something."

"You don't enjoy dancing?"

"I've never had the patience. I like activities with a little more excitement."

"Sports?"

"Yes. All of them. Give me a ball of any kind, and I'm content."

"Then why did you consent to the dance lesson?"

His grin was sheepish. "I did it to impress you."

Something warm and pleasurable blossomed in her soul, and she leaned forward in her chair, her eyes shining. "Since you've gone to all that trouble, I see no reason to waste your efforts." She stood up. "I'm sure I lack some of the more sterling qualities of your mop, but do you think I would be a good substitute?"

"Do you like to live dangerously?"

"Sometimes."

"In that case . . ." He left the fireplace and held his arms out toward her. "May I have this dance?"

He looked so stiff and uncomfortable standing there anticipating the dance that she wanted to smile. But there was something sweet and gentle and humble about him, too, and that made her want to cuddle him against her chest and stroke his hair. He was a much more complex man than she had first imagined.

She slid smoothly into his embrace. He took one awkward step, still moving stiffly as if he had never held a woman in his arms before.

"I'm not fragile, Dan. I won't break."

"It's not you I'm worried about; it's your toes."

"They'll survive, too."

The hauntingly beautiful music played on, lovers' music, just right for cheek-to-cheek dancing and heart-to-heart cuddling. It could have been a washboard band playing "The Old Gray Mare" for all Dan noticed. He'd been born to win, and for him conquering the complicated art of dance was another way to prove to himself that he could excel at anything. Executing the right steps was tantamount to putting points on the scoreboard.

Holding Janet at a distance, barely touching her, his lips began to move. One, two, three, four, he counted silently. Anybody could do the fox-trot.

"Dan."

He missed a step and almost squashed her toe. "Oops. Sorry."

She held back her laughter. "Dancing is not a nine-inning game."

"It has rules, though. I know if I get the moves right I can do this."

"Think of it as a contact sport."

Janet made one deft move that put her in contact with his chest. His arms automatically closed about her.

"There. Isn't that better?"

"Yes." He smiled down at her. "But is it dancing?"

"The best kind." She swayed to the beat of the music. "Feel the rhythm, Dan. Move with it."

"Sideways or backwards?"

"It doesn't matter. Just forget your feet and move with the music."

The stiffness went out of him as he gave himself up to the pleasure of catching Janet's rhythm. It felt so good to him that he exuberantly danced her all the way around the room. She didn't have the heart to tell him that if they had been on a small, crowded dance floor he'd have mowed down six couples on his circuit.

"Hey, this isn't so bad." He pulled her closer and began another enthusiastic dancing tour of the room.

"Coach, the object is not necessarily to cover as much ground as possible."

"What is the object, Doc?"

"To enjoy the pleasure of the music and the pleasure of the one in your arms. Like so." She took the lead and tenderly initiated Dan into the pleasures of slow dancing.

Suddenly dancing fell into place for Dan. It was as if his body had always known what to do if it could get past the stubborn block in his mind. His hands began to caress her back, and his head lowered itself until his face was quite naturally in her fragrant hair.

"Ahh, Doc. This kind of dancing could lead to other things."

"What other things, Coach?"

He chuckled softly. "Is that an invitation for another demonstration?"

She leaned back slightly so she could look directly into his eyes. "I'm not sure I could survive another demonstration with either my sanity or my honor intact."

"Neither could I. Why don't we call a simple truce for the rest of the evening?"

"Agreed."

Cuddled even closer, they continued their slow swaying movements in front of the warm winter fire. She thought he was tender and funny and endearing and enormously, dangerously sexy. That she had once thought him hopelessly old-fashioned now seemed a rash judgment. And she was extraordinarily close to losing her head over him.

He thought she was gorgeous and talented and sweet and heart-stoppingly desirable. That he had ever considered her ridiculously modern seemed a foolish notion to him. And he was dangerously close to losing his heart to her.

When the music ended they slowly drew apart.

"Thank you for the dance, Doc."

"Any time, Coach."

He ran his hands carefully down her arms, as if he were taking her measure for future reference. Then he stepped back.

"I think one good turn deserves another, don't you?"

She smiled. "That's a nice old-fashioned philosophy. But I can go along with it."

"Since you've taught me to dance, I want to share something with you...."

She waited, not knowing what to expect, half hoping he would suggest some outrageous proposition that would continue their game, half hoping he wouldn't.

"Something very important to me." He paused, looking deep into her eyes. "Doc, will you go with me to the soccer game Thursday night?"

"Your team?"

"Yes. The Eagles. We'll be playing our archrivals from West Point, The Mastiffs. Can you come, Janet?"

"What time?"

"Six o'clock. Junior-high games always start early."

It would be difficult, but if she got her associate to take her hospital rounds she could make it.

"I'll be there... unless I have an emergency."

"Wear comfortable clothing and be prepared to do a lot of yelling."

"Why is that?"

He chucked her under the chin. "Doc, I see I have a lot to teach you about ball."

"It has to be easier than baking cookies."

From somewhere in Dan's enormous house, a grandfather clock struck the hour. Eleven o'clock. Time for a working physician to be in bed.

Dan helped her on with her coat and walked her to her car. After he had tucked her inside, he leaned down, took her hand and pressed a warm kiss into her palm.

She felt the pleasure all the way to her toes. Still, she was wary. "A game tactic, Coach?" she asked after he had released her.

"No. A simple kiss between friends." He closed her car door and waved. "Good night, Doc." Then he stood in his driveway watching until her taillight was merely a tiny flicker of red in the distance.

Thursday took forever to come. Or so it seemed to Dan. Fortunately he had been too busy with teaching his classes and getting his team ready for the soccer game to have much time for worrying about Janet.

That evening, standing on the sidelines of the soccer field, he finished giving his team their pregame pep talk and looked up into the bleachers. She wasn't there. That much was certain. The fields at Sportsplex weren't enormous, and with the bright electric lights flooding the area, it wouldn't be that hard to spot one gorgeous auburn-haired female doctor. He scanned the crowd again. Two minutes to game time and Janet was not there. To top it all off, it had started to rain—just a light drizzle, but enough to make the field soggy and the air damp and miserable.

Dan turned back to his team. It wouldn't do to let them see his disappointment. Psychology was an important factor in winning. A positive we-can-win attitude was vital.

"All right, Eagles. Who is going to win this game?"

"We are, Coach." The chorus of excited, enthusiastic voices made him temporarily forget Janet. The game was about to begin. *His* game. *His* team. The teenagers in their navy-and-gold uniforms, with their well-toned young bodies and their eager faces, were depending on him for leadership and guidance. He would not let them down.

"Then let's get out there and *play*."

In the first five minutes of play, The Eagles' goalie, Clint Mark, slipped in the wet grass and West Point scored. From the sideline, Dan cheered his team on.

"That's all right, boys. The game's young. We can do it."

Revitalized by the pep talk, two of his forwards did some dazzling footwork, dribbling the ball toward their goal. Then little Shoeshine Rogers took a headshot, and the ball slammed past West Point's goalie.

The crowd stood up and cheered for the hometown boys. Dan was grateful for the support, and he smiled up into the stands. That's when he spotted her, Dr. Janet Hall, hurrying toward a top-row seat, her green coat open and flapping, revealing a smart blue wool suit. He couldn't tell about her shoes, but judging from the way she was moving she was wearing high heels. Her head was bare, and her dark red hair shone under the stadium lights.

She came, Dan thought. And then, *She's not dressed for the game. She'll catch her death of cold.*

"Coach. Coach." Suddenly he became aware of the voice. Embarrassed, he turned his attention to the young player sitting on the bench. He had been standing in the drizzle staring like some lovesick fool, right in the middle of a game. He'd never been guilty of such lax behavior. He didn't know what had come over him.

"Yes, Bobby?"

"Do you want me to sub for Shoeshine? It looks like he's hurt his foot."

"Yes. And watch out for West Point's Number Three. He's a tough guard."

While the substitution was being made, he risked one more glance into the stands. He thought Janet smiled at him, but at this distance he couldn't be sure.

In the bleachers, Janet *was* smiling at Dan. He looked so right in his baseball cap and his navy jacket that said "Coach Albany," she thought—as much a part of the soccer field as the goalposts and the stadium lights and the bleachers and the hot-dog stand. She couldn't keep her eyes off him. Vitality simply oozed from his pores. She could feel it all the way across the field. And his hair! It was adorably mussed, more so than usual, as if he hadn't had time to do more than run his hands through his dark curls for at least three days. She was so enchanted with her study of him she forgot how cold she was. And how wet.

Around her, the crowd stood up and cheered at intervals. She had no earthly idea what it was all about. The scrambling on the soccer field was totally incomprehensible to her. But no matter. She was seeing Dan at his work, and that made the rushing and last-minute juggling of her schedule worthwhile.

Suddenly a referee blew a whistle, and most of the crowd made a mad dash for the hot-dog stand. With the buffer against the wind gone, Janet shivered.

"You should be wearing a warmer coat and a hat, and I'll bet you haven't had a thing to eat."

She looked up into the bright blue eyes of Coach Dan Albany. In the confusion she hadn't even been aware of his approach.

"I didn't have time for any of that."

"That's what I was afraid of." He sat down on the bleacher beside her. "Here. Hold this." He handed her a soggy hot dog and began to button her coat.

She laughed. "What is all this?"

"Food and pampering. I call it taking care of the doctor."

"Shouldn't you be with your team or something?"

"My assistant is with them. And we're two points ahead. Or haven't you noticed?"

"I can read the scoreboard."

He laughed. "Someday I'm going to teach you this game. But right now..." He fastened the last button on her coat, then took the hot dog from her hand and peeled back the wrapper. "Eat up, Doc."

"Do you know what those things are made of?"

"I never ask. Come on, Doc. Be a good girl and eat something, so I won't feel guilty about dragging you out in the rain with no supper."

"My body will never forgive me for this." She took a big bite, then smiled. "Actually it's not so bad... when you're starving."

Dan grinned. "I'm liable to corrupt you yet." He pulled his baseball cap off and put it on her head, carefully arranging her damp hair away from her face. "When the game is over, Doc, you're supposed to stand up and yell and throw this cap into the air. But be sure you catch it. It's a favorite standby of mine."

"Why am I supposed to do all that?"

"It will be a victory celebration."

"You're that sure of winning?"

He chucked her under the chin. "I always win, Doc."

He left her there in the stands and hurried back to his team.

True to his word, he won the game. By only two points, if she were reading the scoreboard correctly, but nonetheless it was a victory for The Eagles. She stood up with the rest of the crowd and cheered. She even risked throwing Dan's hat in the air, but not very far. She didn't want to lose it. Carefully, she stuffed it into her coat pocket.

Dan came back to her in the thinning crowd.

"How about a private celebration, Doc?"

"Hot chocolate at my house?"

"It's a start." He took her arm and helped her down the bleachers. "Those little pumps you're wearing are impractical. You should keep an old pair of tennis shoes in your car so that at least your feet can be comfortable."

"Is there any special reason I should have tennis shoes in the car . . . other than comfort?"

"For ball games. You ought to throw in an old hooded parka, as well. Weather this time of year can be nasty."

"You sound very certain that I'll be coming to more soccer games."

They were at the bottom of the bleachers now, tagging behind the rest of the fans now rushing toward their cars. He stopped and lifted her chin with one hand. "Won't you, Doc?"

The poignant question hung in the cold air between them. Dan looked so appealingly innocent standing there with his tousled curls and shining eyes, that for an instant she wanted to be an ordinary woman out on a Thursday night date with her favorite man. But that wasn't the case, and she was too smart not to know it. At that moment the burden of her profession seemed almost too much to bear.

Assuming a posture of nonchalance, she smiled at him. "Of course," she said. "I have to prove that I'm your type."

Chapter Seven

Janet drove home in the drizzle, and Dan followed close behind in his pickup truck. When she reached her condominium she hurried inside and waited for Dan with the door held wide.

He shook the rain from his hair before stepping into the light and warmth of her house. "Now that's the kind of welcome home a man likes—a smiling woman, a clean house, and..." He stopped talking and pretended to sniff the air. "What? No aroma of home-baked cookies?"

"I'm smiling because my mouth is permanently frozen in this position; I pay a small fortune to have my house cleaned three times a week, and the cookies are in the pantry in a white baker's bag." Smiling, she held out her hand. "Let me hang your jacket in the closet."

"Not yet. First I have to get you out of your wet clothes." He caught her shoulders and pulled her forward.

She closed her eyes and let the essence of Dan sweep over her—the smell of wet leather, the unexpected gentleness of his big hands, the joyful exuberance that seemed bound in his large body. He flowed through her like a river, wild and turbulent and free. She felt a part of herself being swept along by the tide of his presence—some innocent, romantic part of her being that still believed in the summer magic of carousels and cotton candy and the brass ring that promised "happily ever after."

She felt his hands on her throat, and her eyes snapped open. His eyes were burning down into her face.

"Your skin is cold—" his fingers traced a line from her chin to the point where her skin disappeared into the top of her coat. Slowly he undid the top button "—and much too irresistible." Bending over her he carefully kissed away the raindrops that clung to her throat.

She shivered.

"I'm sorry, Janet. I'm being selfish." Quickly he unbuttoned her wet coat and slid it from her shoulders. Underneath, her wool suit was heavy and damp with rain. "You're soaked."

She chuckled. "You needn't make it sound like I did it deliberately. The rain helped."

He hung her coat in the closet and started to peel off her jacket. The rain had penetrated all the way to her silk blouse, and it clung wetly to her body, the thin fabric molding and shaping her. Dan lost his breath.

For a moment he stood foolishly in the hallway, holding her wool suit jacket halfway off her shoulders, staring down at her as if he had never seen a woman before. Finally, his breath rasped back up in his throat as he took a deep, steadying gulp of air.

"You tempt me almost beyond endurance."

She put her hands on his face. "And you, me."

Their mouths came together in a tight, hungry kiss. He placed one hand in the small of her back and pulled her hard against his chest. Wet, silky fabric clashed with damp leather; soft, feminine curves molded against hard muscles. Their body heat caused the dampness to slowly evaporate, and it rose around them in an almost palpable mist of steam.

Dan bent her backward and she opened herself to him, budding and blossoming like some long-forgotten rose in a tangled, weed-choked flower garden. His hand moved upward into her hair. Taking hold of a silky mass he imprisoned her, taming her movements to match his own.

And when it was over, they stood back from each other panting.

"I shouldn't have come here tonight, Doc." His voice, still raspy with passion, broke the silence that surrounded them.

"I invited you."

"Then you shouldn't have."

"Why not?"

"Because I can't seem to play this game anymore."

"Was it ever a game, Dan?"

"I'm not sure." He reached out and tenderly twined one of her damp curls around his finger. "All I know is that I've got you under my skin, and I can't seem to do anything about it."

"Do you want me to prescribe a cure?"

"Can you?"

"No. I'm not good at matters of the heart."

"I'm not sure that I am, either." He released the curl and smoothed her hair back from her face. "I used to think I was. I used to believe in myself as a Saturday afternoon matinee idol, some bigger-than-life hero who knew exactly what he wanted in a woman."

"And now?"

"And now..." His hands slowly memorized her face. "I think I'm falling in love with you."

She stood still under the lovely flowing rhythm of his hands, waiting for him to say more, waiting for her own tumultuous emotions to become sane and ordered.

"Dan..."

"Shhh." He pressed his index finger over her lips. "You don't have to say anything. I know you're too sensible to ever fall for a man whose life is measured by points on a scoreboard."

His words hurt. She didn't take the time to analyze the reasons; she acted on instinct.

"And of course you're far too smart to become seriously involved with a woman whose career might preempt a game or two."

He was stung by her vehemence. "Janet, is that what you think of me? That I'm so shallow I put sports ahead of friends and family?"

"Why shouldn't I make that judgment? You've already decided I'm too narrow to make room for anything in my life except medicine."

They stepped back from each other, as tense as two boxers on opposite sides of the ring. Bright spots of color rode high on Janet's cheeks. Dan felt a small muscle twitch in his own stubborn jaw. He longed to reach for her, to bridge the gap with one passionate, all-consuming kiss.

Finally Janet spoke.

"I think you'd better go, Coach."

"I can't leave you like this."

"Like what?"

Hurt, he wanted to say. *Angry.* Instead, he chose an easier way out.

"Wet."

"Wet?"

"Yes. You're liable to take a cold and I'll feel responsible."

"You can leave with a clear conscience, Coach. I plan to drink two glasses of orange juice. Vitamin C."

His smile was tinged with sadness. "I would have prescribed a warm brandy, a cozy fire and lots of cuddling."

"That just goes to show you how unsuitable we are for each other. We don't see eye to eye on anything."

"You're right." Instinctively he reached out to touch her. With his hand hovering in the air halfway to her cheek, he changed his mind. Endings were best done quickly. There was less pain that way. "Good night, Doc. Thanks for coming to my game."

She almost said, *Any time.* But all that was behind them now, the easy camaraderie, the fun and games, the quick, bright passions.

"You're welcome." Her words were stiff with tightly controlled anger and more than a little heartache.

Dan stood uncertainly a moment longer; then he turned and walked out, taking care to close the door softly.

She walked to the door and almost called him back. Instead she leaned her head against the cool wood and closed her eyes. "It's best this way," she whispered.

Outside, Dan placed his hand on the doorknob. He almost turned and went back inside. Then he changed his mind.

"It would never have worked," he muttered to himself. As pep talks went, it rated as his worst. His heart was heavy as he climbed into his pickup truck and drove to his big, rambling house on Church Street.

The next day Janet told herself that she had been wise to show Dan the door. It was best to break off before things became too serious. She didn't want another Guy Maxwell. What Dan had said about her being too smart to fall for a coach was almost the same thing Guy had said when he broke their engagement—that her profession automatically shut her out of meaningful relationships. At least she hadn't let things get that far with Dan. There had been no promises made, no commitments uttered, no love pledged.

She had been smart. Wise. Sophisticated. Then why did she feel so wretched? She glanced down at her watch. Only 11:00 a.m. and already the day felt a thousand hours long. When there was nothing to look forward to at the end of the day, life was like that; an endless procession of minutes and hours that had to be dealt with.

Sighing, she picked up the chart on her desk. Another patient was waiting—little Becky Skaggs who had come in for her allergy shots, no doubt. There were always her patients. And she had Harvey. She had to remember that.

Putting on a professional smile, she rose from her desk and went through the door that connected her office to examining room number one.

"Well now, Becky. What can I do for you today?"

"I breaved dust balls and got all red and itchy."

"I know just how to fix that problem, Becky."

She selected a disposable syringe from her supply cabinet and began to fill it with a dose of Becky's allergy medication. And so she would fill the day, she thought, dispensing shots and pills and soothing words of advice. And all the other days of her life.

It was only eleven in the morning, and already Dan had lost his concentration for the sixteenth time. Several students in the back of the classroom tittered. Dan had no idea what he had said to cause such hilarity.

Blaming his bad day on the fact that it was Friday, he faced his students.

"Turn to page sixty-five and we'll continue our study of love triangles."

The class erupted in laughter. If Dan had been a man given to puzzlement, he'd have scratched his head in wonder. As it was he fixed a stern blue gaze on the students.

"I hope all of you find the study of triangles this funny on exam day."

A brave soul in the back of the room raised his hand.

"Question, Brick?"

"What kind of triangles, Coach Hall? Isosceles or love?"

One of Dan's finer qualities was the ability to laugh at himself.

"In the spring a young man's fancy turns to love . . . and an old man's, too," he quipped. "Spring is not so far away. I guess I'm a few months ahead of schedule. Or a few years behind." He glanced at the big clock on his classroom wall. Five minutes to bell time. "Take a break, class. You can use the last five minutes to study or chat—or even to flirt, if you keep it reasonable."

An hour later Dr. Michelle Leonard cornered him in the cafeteria.

"Love triangles, Coach Hall?"

Grinning, he scooted down and made room for her at his table. "Word even got to the principal's ivory tower, did it?"

"You know what they say about juicy school gossip. Faster than a speeding bullet." She unfolded her paper napkin and spread it on her lap. "I hope this means that you and my friend Janet Hall are hitting it off."

"She's a friend of yours?"

"The best. We were undergraduates together. Although we don't have that much time to spend together now, we still keep up. So . . . you didn't comment. How are you two getting along?''

"Wonderful. Terrible. It depends on your point of view."

"Aha."

"What does 'aha' mean?"

"It means you've finally met a woman who rings your chimes."

He assumed a severe posture. "Dr. Leonard, didn't they teach you in graduate school not to use clichés?"

"If the cliché fits, wear it. That's what I always say." She put down her fork and half turned in her seat so that she could give him her undivided attention.

"She's a brilliant, dedicated doctor, but don't make the same mistake most men do. Don't underestimate her potential for a warm and loving relationship."

Something inside Dan went very still and watchful. He pushed aside his tray and stared at Michelle. "Be specific, Michelle. What other men?"

"You're not the jealous type, are you, Dan?" She smiled at him, then patted his face. "No. I thought not. It's no secret that Guy Maxwell was the one who broke off their engagement. He claimed she had no time for anything except her career."

"Damn fool."

"Right."

"I was thinking about myself." He glanced at his watch. "Damn."

Michelle was always sensitive to the needs of her teachers, and she was especially interested in this case since two of her good friends were involved.

"Dan, if you need to leave early I can teach your afternoon classes."

"You're sure?"

"Positive. Besides, it will do me good to get out of my ivory tower and see how the peons live." She swatted his leg. "Scoot."

"The lesson plans are in the top drawer, left side."

Dan didn't scoot, but he did stride. Within five minutes he was in the principal's office signing an early-leave form.

"Coach Hall?" Michelle's secretary, Barbara West, came toward him with a slip of paper in her hand. "This message came for you fifteen minutes ago."

He read the message and began to smile. "This is exactly the excuse I need." He bent down and gave Barbara a hearty kiss on the cheek. "Thanks, Barb."

She flushed beet-red. "Well, my goodness. Goodness, gracious me." Her hands fluttered to her cheeks. "Well, gracious sakes alive. That's what I'm here for. To take messages."

She "gracious saked" for two more minutes, but there was nobody to hear her. Dan Albany had long since gone out the door.

By two-thirty that afternoon, Janet was weary.

"Eleanor," she said to the nurse who assisted in her clinic, "how many more patients do I have this afternoon?"

"I'll check."

Five minutes later she was back in Janet's office. "You only have one scheduled. Bronwyn Clements."

"Good. I need to get to the hospital early today."

"There's a man who has come in insisting that you see one more patient."

"Did you recommend Dr. Lawrence to him?"

"I did, but he says he can't see anyone else." Eleanor smiled. "He's quite handsome, and extremely persuasive. I'm afraid Julie and I were putty in his hands."

"You didn't!"

"I did. I told him to get his patient and wait in examining room two."

"He didn't have the child?"

"No. The boy was waiting in the car."

"In the car! I'll have something to say to him about that." Janet made a final notation on the chart in front of her, then smiled at Eleanor. "And I'll deal with you and my gullible receptionist later."

"We're quaking in our boots."

"You don't wear boots, Eleanor." She made a waving motion with her hand. "Shoo." As the nurse reached the door, Janet said, "The new patient, Eleanor. What is his name?"

"Harvey."

She thought Eleanor was grinning when she said it, but the nurse disappeared through the door too quickly for her to find out more. Harvey. It couldn't be. Janet glanced down at her watch. Two-thirty. Dan was still at Graden Junior High. And anyway, what possible reason would he have for coming to her clinic—and bringing Harvey? They'd said everything that needed to be said last night.

She dismissed the idea as ridiculous and went in to see Bronwyn Clements. Bronwyn was a bright, bouncy, happy baby who needed nothing more than her booster shots. Janet chatted with her mother a moment about the proper kinds of baby food, then headed for examining room two.

When she pushed open the door the first thing she saw was Harvey, dressed in a hospital gown, his big pink tongue lolling out the side of his mouth and his heavy tail thumping the paper on the examining table.

"Harvey!" Laughing, she walked across the room and embraced the dog. "You great big mutt. When did you get out of the hospital?"

"Just this afternoon." Dan, who had been sitting in a chair hidden behind the door, stood up. He was smiling over the top of an enormous bouquet of roses—red, pink, white and yellow, all jumbled together in a flamboyant riot of color and spreading their rich fragrance throughout the room. He held the flowers out to her. "Peace offering."

Forgiveness came easily for Janet, and a brightness suddenly entered her day. She felt as if she could see fifteen more patients and single-handedly produce a cure for the common cold. The sudden buoyancy of her spirit was screaming evidence of Dan's effect on her.

She wasn't entirely sure that she wanted her emotions and her spirit to be that closely tied up with a man—any man. Her independence was threatened. And yet... Happiness this great had to be worth some sacrifices.

She stood so long staring at him and his roses that Dan began to get a little worried. Well, he thought, what had he expected? That she would tumble into his arms like some pigtailed sixteen-year-old? After all, she was a doctor, and he had been a perfect jackass last night.

He kept his grin in place, hoping it was rakish enough to hide the fact that his heart was trying to hammer its way out of his chest. He wasn't going to let her silence daunt him. After all, he was accustomed to winning.

"Well, Doc. Aren't you going to take the roses? I was nearly picked up by men with nets and carted off to Whitfield getting them for you. The florist thought I couldn't make up my mind about the color, and then she didn't understand that a dozen wouldn't do. She said nobody had ever placed such an order and she wasn't even sure how to charge for it. And then—"

"Dan."

"What?"

"I love the roses."

"That's a relief. For a minute there I thought you were going to bash me over the head with them."

"The thought crossed my mind." She took the enormous bouquet and buried her face in the sweet-smelling petals. When she looked back at him, she was smiling. "When you set out to win a game, you do it with style, Coach."

The rakish grin disappeared from his face as he strode toward her. Cupping her cheeks with his warm hands, he gazed deep into her eyes. "The game is over, Doc."

"Is it?" she whispered.

"Yes." His thumbs caressed her chin. "It's just you and me now, a man and a woman with totally incompatible professions and wildly different life-styles. Two people who will have to muddle through the best we can. Two people only a hair's breadth away from being in love."

"You're presuming I feel the same way."

"Not presuming, Janet. Knowing." Watching her reaction, he gently traced the planes of her cheekbones, outlined the shape of her lips. "I *know* that you feel the same excitement I do when we touch. And when we kiss... ah, Janet..." He closed his eyes for a moment, and when he opened them they were so bright that looking into them almost hurt her eyes. "When we kiss, I think the angels bend down from heaven in envy."

"Dan, you have the soul of a poet."

"Didn't I tell you? I love the romantics... Wordsworth, Shelley, Keats and Byron."

"I didn't know."

"There are other things you don't know about me. And there's much I don't know about you." His finger traced back and forth over her lips again. "Janet, let's learn each other."

"No games?"

"None."

She stalled. Was she willing to risk another commitment, another try at love, another heartbreak? "Playing games with you was fun."

"We can have the fun without the games."

"Dan—" she gazed into his eyes until she almost drowned in their blueness "—I'm willing to try."

His sigh of relief was genuine. "I thought you'd never say that."

"So did I."

"I know about Guy, Janet. I'm sorry—sorry he hurt you, and even sorrier that I did."

"How did you know?"

"Our mutual friend, Michelle Leonard."

"I'm not sure how I feel about her telling you."

He smiled. "Feel good about it, Doc. I love a woman with a past. It makes you mysterious."

"And I love a man who is willing to be declared insane over a bouquet of roses."

Harvey, who had grown tired of thumping his tail and being ignored, woofed from his perch on the table.

They both laughed.

"Harvey agrees with you, Doc."

Holding the armful of roses, she went to the examining table and put one hand on the dog's head. "Speaking of Harvey, I want to know how you managed to get past my receptionist *and* my nurse. Eleanor is usually formidable."

"That's one of the things you should know about me— I'm irresistible to women."

"There's one thing you should know about me, Coach. I don't like sharing."

"Then you have nothing to worry about. When I fall in love, I'll be the most loyal, serious, one-woman man you ever saw."

When I fall in love. The phrase sang through her mind with a lovely heart-lifting lilt. Dan made it all sound so easy. But she wasn't quite ready to believe yet. So she changed the subject.

"What did the vet say about Harvey? And how did you ever get him into this ridiculous gown?"

"You always do that."

"Do what?"

"Ask two questions at the same time."

"I suppose it's because I usually *do* two things at the same time. I do most of my medical reading while I'm in the tub."

"I can think of more exciting uses for the tub."

She came very close to blushing. "You didn't answer my questions."

Dan loved seeing the high color in her cheeks, loved the idea that he had put it there, loved the lively give-and-take of their conversations, loved the underlying current of passion that was always between them.

He smiled at Janet, and when he did the whole room seemed brighter for his happiness.

"Nurse Eleanor graciously helped with the gown. And except for that scar on his leg, Harvey is back to his usual exuberant self. He can't wait to get back to a home-cooked dinner of hot dogs and pizza and cream-filled cupcakes."

"Dan Albany, don't you dare. He needs proper nutrition to continue the healing process and to maintain his health."

"Spoken like a doctor."

"I am."

"I know, and I'm beginning to enjoy this doctorly side of you. But I enjoy the passionate side more." In three strides he was at her side, plucking the roses from her hand and putting them in the small sink beside the examining table. Then he swept her into his arms. "Doc, it's been too long since I kissed you."

The kiss was a healing, forgiving, welcome-home joining that was both sweet and tender. Dan carefully held his passion in check. Now was not the time for hot longing and out-of-control desire. Now was the time to let his lips say "I care for you. I want to know you, to understand you." And so he kissed with exquisite tenderness.

Janet felt as if she had been locked inside a helium-filled balloon and turned loose in a sparkling summer sky. Joy bubbled through her veins, and she was intoxicated by the wonder of this man she held in her arms.

She was reluctant to let go.

So was he.

They might have kissed forever if Harvey hadn't decided to get in on the act. He nudged his big head against Dan's side and began to lick his arm.

Dan was smiling when he lifted his hand. "I think somebody wants some attention."

"I think somebody wants out of that gown."

Together they undressed Harvey and got him off the examining table. And then they made plans.

"I'll take Harvey to my house. It's bigger than your condo, and I have a fenced-in backyard where he can get plenty of exercise."

"That's sensible."

"He'll expect his favorite doctor to make house calls."

"He will?"

"I will, too."

"I'm glad you said that."

"So am I."

They stood grinning self-consciously at each other. Dan cleared his throat.

"Do you like movies, Doc?"

"Yes."

Dan's grin was huge. "That's fantastic. I love movies."

Janet smiled. "Are you asking me for a date?"

"I am. And doing it badly."

"But with charm."

"Let's go on a real, honest-to-goodness Friday night date, Doc. Just the two of us with bags of popcorn and lots of butter and icy drinks that never taste as good anywhere else as they do in a dark theater. What do you say?"

"I'm doing some tests on a patient of mine in the hospital. And then I have rounds. Can we make it a late movie?"

"I'll pick you up at your condo. Nine?"

"That sounds good."

"I'll see you later, then."

Dan took Harvey's leash and started to leave. When he reached the door, he turned back to her. "Janet—"

She smiled, waiting.

Dan hesitated, feeling as foolish and tongue-tied as a pimply-faced teenager at his first dance. Now that he had stopped, he wasn't even sure what he wanted to say. There were a million things that *needed* saying: *This time it will be different. I'll handle you with great care. Forgive me for the hurt. We'll make it work.* But now didn't seem the right time or place.

And so he said, "You look good in white."

Smiling, she spread her lab coat wide. "This old thing? It's just something I picked up with my degree."

"It suits you."

He waved, and then he was gone.

Janet stood a moment longer, savoring the feel of Dan that seemed to permeate examining room two. It was remarkable that he was somehow able to imbue a place with his presence so that even when he was gone, it seemed that he still lingered there.

Finally she roused herself to action. Going to the door she called her nurse. Eleanor came down the hall grinning.

Janet assumed a severe tone. "Well, Eleanor, you think all that was pretty funny, huh?"

"We had the devil of a time getting that big dog in that little hospital gown. All those roses kept getting in the way."

Janet chuckled. "It *was* pretty funny. Dan looked so much like a little boy, standing behind that door holding that enormous bouquet." She lifted the roses out of the sink. "Help me get all these in water, Eleanor. I'm already late for the hospital."

Eleanor took a handful of roses. "But, oh my. Wasn't he worth it?"

Janet stared thoughtfully into space a moment, remembering. "Yes. Ahh, yes."

Chapter Eight

Dan and Janet slid into empty back row theater seats just as the late movie was beginning. She hadn't had time to change out of her suit and high heels, but Dan was wearing a comfortable-looking red wool sweater under his leather jacket, and jogging shoes that looked as if they were familiar with forest paths, mud holes and grassy creek banks. When he settled back in his seat, he looked as relaxed as if he'd been there all evening.

She envied his capacity for relaxation. Her neck was stiff with tension and her stomach was clenched in a knot. She couldn't get Randy Sanderford off her mind. She'd ordered another brain scan on him this afternoon.

Suddenly she felt Dan's hand on her neck, his fingers warm and strong, stroking, massaging, *caring*. She closed her eyes and leaned back.

"How did you know I needed that?" Although the back two rows of seats were empty, she kept her voice quiet.

"Instinct." He scooted down in his seat so that his head would be on a level with hers. "You don't come to the movies often, do you?"

"I think the last movie I saw in a theater was an old Esther Williams swimming extravaganza."

"Doc, I'm just what you need." His hand stopped its wonderful massage and slid down to cup her right shoulder. With gentle pressure he eased her head down into the crook of his arm. "Can you still see the screen?"

"Yes." It was the truth, but she wouldn't have cared if she hadn't been able to see a thing. Sitting in the dark theater with the smells of buttery popcorn all around and her head on Dan's shoulder was exactly what she needed at the moment. She wished she could bottle the feeling and dispense it to her patients.

"You just stay right there. I'm going to take good care of you." He reached into the big cardboard tub of popcorn that was sitting in his lap and took a handful of buttery morsels. "Open wide." One by one, he popped them into her mouth.

Butter drizzled down his fingers. Feeling relaxed and pampered and reckless, she took his forefinger in her mouth and sucked away the butter.

"Ahh, Doc. Keep that up and I won't be responsible for what I do."

Grinning wickedly she stroked his finger with her tongue. He took his finger out of her mouth and traced her lips. Then he leaned over and nibbled away the salty, buttery moisture.

Oblivious to the movie, they fed each other popcorn.

"You get butter in the nicest places," she whispered as she leaned over to kiss his chin.

"A little bit lower, Doc."

"Here?" She pressed her tongue briefly on the pulse point at the base of his throat.

"Indeed." He groaned softly. "Ahh, Janet. How hungry you make me."

"I can remedy that."

She fed him another handful of popcorn, lingering to caress his lips with her fingertips.

His eyes shone in the darkness. "Hungry for you, Janet."

"I'm sure it's a temporary condition."

"I'm not sure I want it to be."

Looking deep into each other's eyes, they both reached into the popcorn tub at the same time. It was empty. Their hands touched, and their fingers entwined.

"Neither am I," she whispered.

They stayed that way for a small eternity, searching for answers to questions they dared not ask. Finally, hands still locked inside the greasy popcorn tub, they both turned back to the screen.

The vast green cornfields of Iowa spread out before them on the wide screen, and the larger-than-life actors spoke of dreams, of knowing them, nurturing them, and not letting them pass by unheeded.

In the darkness, Dan's quiet voice came to her. "What are your dreams, Janet?"

"To ease suffering, to heal."

"That's professional. What about your personal dreams?"

"I . . . haven't thought about them in a long, long time." She swiveled her head so she could see his face. "What about you, Dan. Do you dream?"

"Yes. I have my dream house and my dream dog. I used to have a clear picture of my future, but the shape of it keeps changing lately." He lifted her hand to his lips and kissed away all the remnants of butter. "I'm not sure what my dream is anymore."

"I'm glad."

He smiled. "You are?"

"Yes." Seeing the intensity in his face, she suddenly realized that she wasn't ready to encourage him to dream new dreams, to consider her as a part of his future. Nor was she yet ready to consider him. There was too much between them that had to be worked out. And so she sought to bring their relationship back to a more casual level. "Daring to change your dreams shows that you have an open mind, and an open mind is a sign of great intelligence."

He chuckled. "I don't think that was exactly what I wanted to hear, but I guess I can live with that for a while."

The movie ended and the crowd began to disperse. Dan and Janet stayed in their seats rather than join the press of people in the aisles.

"What do you do for exercise, Janet?"

She grinned at him. "How do you know I exercise?"

"It's the body, Doc." He leaned back, lifting his eyebrows and leering at her with mock lasciviousness. "Anyway, a woman as health conscious as you is bound to do something," he added.

"I jog."

"So do I. We'll jog together in the morning."

She laughed. "How do you know?"

"Because I'm the kind of guy who won't take no for an answer."

"What time?"

"I'm flexible. You name it."

"Early. I have to be at the clinic at eight-thirty."

"On Saturday?"

"Children get sick on weekends, too. We're open until noon, and I'm not on call every weekend."

"Six-thirty, then."

"Your place or mine?"

"Mine. Harvey is lonesome to see you."

"How do you know?"

"Man talk. We understand each other."

Dan and Janet left the theater, and he drove her home. They kept up the lighthearted banter all the way back to her condominium. He parked by her Porsche and escorted her to her door.

She was quivering inside, not from the cold but from need. In the space of one week Dan Albany had become a warm and vital presence in her life, and she wasn't sure she knew what to do about it. She shivered.

"Cold?" He turned her coat collar up around her chin and then cupped her face.

"It's getting late."

"So it is." He leaned down and kissed her quickly, for he knew that he was in no condition to kiss deeply and walk away. "Good night, Doc. See you in the morning."

She lifted her hand in small farewell as he walked back to his pickup. "See you."

He turned for one last smile, blew her a kiss, then climbed into his truck and drove away.

She went inside her empty house. "See you," she whispered.

Dan was waiting for her when she got to his house the next morning.

He bounded down his front steps and helped her from her car. "You look smashing, Doc."

She smiled, genuinely pleased by his compliment. "Why, thank you."

"Turn around." He took her hand and gently spun her around. "I've never seen you in casual clothes and I want to feast my eyes. Yes, indeed. You'll do nicely."

She laughed. "Do for what?"

"At the moment, jogging. What do you prefer, the sidewalks or a regular track?"

"It's such a lovely morning, why don't we use the streets. I love to see the neighborhood this time of morning."

"Great. I'll adjust my pace to yours."

He closed her car door, and they started jogging south on Church Street. To his delight, she didn't slow him down at all. She had the long legs of a tall woman and was obviously in excellent form. They turned west on Jefferson and jogged down past the library, past her condo and all the stately old homes that were a part of Tupelo's quiet charm and Southern heritage. With their breath making white clouds in the still morning air, they set a smart pace past his school and up Robins Street where small bungalows had been restored with loving care by Tupelo's young married set. They turned back east on Jackson Street, still not winded, past the football stadium, then south again on Church until they were back at his house.

"Thanks for the workout, Dan." Janet started for her car.

He took her hand. "Whoa there, Doc. I'll bet you haven't had breakfast yet."

"Not yet."

"Then you're in for a treat." He took her hand and led her up his front walk and into his house. Stopping in the hallway, he hung their jogging jackets on the hall tree.

"Come with me, Doc."

Laughing, she followed him. "I'm not used to taking orders."

"I'm used to giving them. I promise you, obeying will be painless."

He tucked her hand in the crook of his elbow and led her into his kitchen. It was a large, airy room with huge bay windows that let in the early morning light, tall ceilings hung with racks of brass pots and pans, and glass-fronted cabinets filled with a mixture of antique depression-glass plates, heavy pewter mugs and handmade pottery wineglasses. A big iron restaurant stove stood in one corner, and an oak claw-foot table sat in gleaming splendor underneath the windows.

"This is where I do my dastardly deeds. Sit right here." He led her to a chair beside the table. Harvey came padding in from his rug beside the fireplace and laid his head on Janet's lap.

"Wish I could do that, Doc."

She rubbed the dog behind his big, silky ears. "If you did, we might both starve to death."

"I'd be willing to make the sacrifice."

"I would, too—some other time. I have patients waiting."

"In that case, we'll have to postpone the cuddling until . . . tonight, Janet?"

"Yes, Dan. I want to see you tonight."

He gave her a happy grin, then turned his attention to preparing breakfast. He whistled while he worked. Janet sat back in her chair and relaxed. Dan's kitchen was warm and cozy and cheerful, and sitting there watching him prepare a high-cholesterol, high-fat, starch-laden meal was infinitely better than being in her kitchen alone with her fruit and cereal. Of course, she thought, as she watched him break eggs into the skillet, that kind of diet was bad for his heart. But she'd talk to him about diet later. Right now she didn't want to do anything to spoil the wonderful mood.

She set the table, with Harvey demanding much attention and getting in the way. She and Dan laughed a lot, and ate a lot and talked a lot—about their plans for the evening, about education and politics and science and, surprisingly, poetry. It was Harvey who started that conversation.

He curled himself into a contented ball and lay at Dan's feet, his tail thumping against the polished tiles.

Dan looked down at him and quoted, " 'I think I could turn and live with animals, they are so placid and self-contain'd...' "

Janet smiled at him in surprise. "Walt Whitman."

"Yes. From 'Song of Myself.' "

She leaned her elbows on the table and gazed at him. "Dan Albany, you continue to surprise me."

"Do you like surprises, Janet?"

"Yes. Not as a steady diet, but enough to make life interesting."

He took her hand and kissed it. "I'm beginning to see that it's the differences in people and not their sameness that makes life wonderful."

"If this is a courtship, Dan, it's beautiful."

"Thank you."

"As much as I hate to leave, I must." He stood up and pulled out her chair. She brushed his cheek with her fingertips. "See you tonight."

"I'll walk you to your car." They stopped by the hall tree for her jogging jacket, and then he escorted her out. "Take care, Doc."

"You, too."

Dan didn't want to watch her leave. He hurried back inside to his kitchen where Harvey waited. "Didn't she liven this place up, old boy?" Harvey whined his agreement. "Did you see the way the sunlight streaked her hair? It looked like flame. That woman inspires me to poetry, boy." He began to clear the breakfast dishes. "I think it's love,

Harvey." Harvey woofed. "Why, thank you. When you fall in love, I'll offer my congratulations, too."

After Dan had stacked his dishes in the dishwasher, he let Harvey out into the backyard to get some sunshine. He had just come back in when the phone rang.

It was Betty June.

"Dan, I'm desperate."

Dan wasn't alarmed. Betty June was given to drama.

"Tell me what's wrong. Maybe I can help you."

"Would you? I knew I could count on you."

"Count on me for what, Betty June?"

"To baby-sit. You see, Ron and I were watching this special about Andrew Wyeth on educational TV and he got this brilliant idea to drive up to Memphis today to see the Rodin exhibit. You know how these art history professors are. Well, we haven't been anywhere in three months, and . . . anyway, I called Peg in Pontotoc, but she's going to run a booth at her church's winter bazaar and so I thought of you. I hope I'm not interrupting your plans."

Dan thought of his plans, and it was on the tip of his tongue to tell his sister that he couldn't baby-sit. Then he thought about her life, how she and Ron stayed home most of the time, attending school and church functions that involved their children. And how they so seldom went anywhere because they couldn't find a sitter for their four lively offspring.

"Bring them over, Sis. I'll be glad to do it." Janet would understand. She might even want to come over and visit. That idea perked him up considerably.

"You're an angel, Dan."

"Dress them for the outdoors. I'll take them to soccer practice this afternoon."

After he had hung up Dan glanced at his watch. Janet would still be at the clinic. He didn't want to call and interrupt her work, especially with bad news. Would she consider a broken date bad news? He selfishly hoped so.

He picked up a dust mop and tackled the monumental task of dusting his knickknacks. The duster was old and ragged, and amidst the fog of loose feathers and dust, Dan decided that he would stop by Janet's condo on his way to soccer practice and tell her in person about the change in plans. That sounded good to him—change in plans. Better than breaking a date. It also left the way open for him to include her in the new plans.

By the time Betty June arrived with the children, Dan was feeling chipper about the turn of events. He loved children, especially his niece and nephews, and he wanted Janet to know and love them, too. Now was a good time for that.

After Betty June had gone, Dan involved the children in a romp in the backyard. Butch and Samuel, budding engineers that they were, immediately took their pails and tin shovels and started digging a hole to China. Peter played a game of catch with his Uncle Dan, while Merry, the botanist, collected dead leaves and discovered Harvey's sudden romance.

"Look, Uncle Dan," she called from the west side of the yard. "Harvey's got a girlfriend."

Dan looked up in time to see his dog prancing and preening in front of the clapboard fence. His audience was visible between the wooden slats—a standard poodle, resplendent in pink ribbons and a pink doggie jacket.

"Gwendolyn," the poodle's owner called. "Gwendolyn, come away from that fence." A fat little woman with a red pouty mouth and yellow store-bought curls that bounced like sausages around her face snapped a leash on Gwendolyn and led her away, chiding all the while, "Bad doggie.

You know that big mutt next door doesn't have a pedigree. Bad girl.''

Dan and Peter burst out laughing, and Merry said, "Uncle Dan, what's a Pet Agree?"

Dan explained about bloodlines, and by the time he had finished, the children were hungry. He fed them lunch, got the sleepy twins into bed for a quick nap, and took down some board games for Peter and Merry. Then he settled down to watch the clock.

Janet would be home soon—barring emergencies. He crossed his fingers and fervently prayed for the good health of all the children in Tupelo.

Janet was at her desk, writing an article for a medical journal, when the doorbell rang. Laying her reading glasses atop her work, she went to the front door.

"Dan!" Her quick pleasure at seeing him was obvious in her face. He took that as a good sign. She hadn't seen the children yet, though, for they were suddenly shy at the thought of paying a social call to the doctor who gave them shots, and were hiding behind him. "What an unexpected pleasure."

"I hope you'll still think so when you see the rest of your company." He stepped aside and urged the children forward. "My niece and nephews, Merry, Peter, Butch and Samuel."

"The Mayhew children. I should have known when you mentioned your sister, Betty June." Smiling, Janet leaned down and took Peter's hand. "How are you, Peter?"

"Good, Dr. Hall. I don't need a shot and neither does Merry." He put his arm protectively around his sister. Little Butch looked at his pediatrician and began to squall.

Dan scooped him up and patted him soothingly on the bottom. "It's okay, little man. Doctor Hall is our friend."

Janet ushered the children through the door. "Come in out of the cold." They pressed against Dan's legs, staring shyly at Janet's polished floors and gleaming crystal vases.

"I've never seen them this quiet. Do you have a magic wand somewhere on your person, Doc?"

"No. They're merely associating me with sickness and pain. It's a hazard of my profession."

Dan's high hopes for a spontaneous family evening began to wane. Obviously he couldn't take four kids and their doctor and make them into instant friends and bosom buddies. He also noticed Janet's reserve. Maybe she didn't even like kids—except the sick ones. It was a depressing thought.

"We can't stay, Doc. We're on the way to soccer practice."

"All of you?"

"Yes. My assistant will be there today, and everybody on the team will be vying for the chance to play with these little tykes." He set the now-quiet Butch on his feet and picked up Samuel, who was looking teary-eyed and uncertain. "I just came by to tell you that I'll have to change our plans for this evening—and to apologize. Betty June called me this morning and..." He paused, trying to think of the best way to explain why he let his sister's need preempt their plans.

"There's no need for an apology, nor for an explanation." She glanced from Dan to the children. He had never looked more dear to her. His dark hair, forever mussed, was more tousled than usual and his blue eyes were shining with love for the children. He stood watching her expectantly, the expression on his face both yearning and hopeful. What did he want of her? What could she give? She had dealt with children all morning, many of them cranky. She didn't relish the idea of spending the rest of her day with kids. And yet, these weren't just any children; they were Dan's kin. She took a deep breath. "Why don't you leave the children with me while you have soccer practice, Dan?"

Dan sensed that her heart wasn't in the invitation. Anyhow, that wasn't why he had come. "No. It's sunny today and fairly warm. The outing will do them good. And if it gets too cold, I'll leave the practice with Wayne." He bent over Merry. "Button your coat, sweetheart." Then he straightened back up to face Janet. "About tonight—I thought maybe we could rent movies, and you could come over to watch them with us."

"That sounds like fun, Dan, but actually I do need to finish an article I'm writing."

"I'll call you, Janet." He gathered his children and started for the door.

"I'll be waiting."

In the doorway he gave a small wave and then he was gone, the door closing softly behind him.

Janet leaned against the door. Why had she turned him down? It wasn't that she didn't like children. It wasn't even that she didn't want to be with the Mayhew children.

She went back to her desk and sat down. It was true what she had told him. She *did* need to finish writing the article. And yet that wasn't the only reason she had said no. Twirling her glasses in her hand, she stared into space. Dan expected too much of her, she decided. Too much, too soon. She remembered a conversation they had had. "I plan to have a large family," he had said. "Eight. Two parents, six kids."

He had to be...what? Thirty-nine? Forty? That was okay for a man planning a large family. But she was no spring chicken. Far too old to bear six children. And besides, how could she possibly manage a medical career and six children?

She leaned her head on her hands. "Oh, Dan. Have you really changed your dream, or are you hoping I'll change mine?"

The whispered question hung in the air, and there was no one to answer her. In order for love to flourish, two people had to have a common goal, a common vision for the future. That much Janet believed. And she wanted love to flourish between them. She wanted it so much that her heart ached with need. She wanted the laughter, the passion, the friendship, even the tears.

But she also wanted and needed her career. Slowly she put her glasses back on and turned her attention to the paper she was writing. But in the back of her mind she could still see a big man with a charming smile and four little children.

Chapter Nine

After soccer practice Dan took the children to McDonald's, their favorite restaurant, and then they rented three Walt Disney movies.

Back in his house on Church Street, they all settled in for an evening of movie watching. *Cinderella* was a big favorite with the children, but Harvey loved *Bambi* best. All his hunting instincts came out, and he pranced and postured around the room, sniffing and whining at the television screen, and looking so ridiculous that Dan and the children couldn't watch the show for laughing at him.

They took a popcorn and let-off-steam break at eight o'clock. Little Samuel fell asleep, his curly head nodding down toward his plastic popcorn bowl, and Dan carried him off to bed. Afterward Dan and the other three children settled back around the television set and he put the last tape into the VCR.

Halfway through *Snow White* little Butch began to complain.

"Uncah Dan, I feel funny."

Dan leaned over the child and felt his forehead. He'd had enough experience with Betty June's children to know how a feverish child felt. Butch didn't feel hot. "Do you hurt somewhere, Butch?"

"No."

Dan had also had enough experience to realize that finding out a child's ailment took extensive detective work and infinite patience.

"Does your head feel funny?"

"A little."

"Does your stomach hurt?"

"No. It growls."

"I'm going to let you lie on the couch while I get a cool cloth for your head." He tucked a coverlet around the small child and placed him on the sofa. Harvey padded over and lay down on the floor beside the little boy, whining his sympathy. Then Dan went to his bathroom for a cool, wet cloth. By the time he got back into the den, Butch was bending over, vomiting on Harvey. Merry and Peter were squealing with excitement and Harvey was looking a bit insulted.

It took Dan twenty minutes to clean up the mess and get Butch into bed. Meanwhile Peter and Merry and a newly scrubbed Harvey had lost interest in the proceedings and settled back down to watching the movie.

Dan kept a close vigil on Butch, and an hour later when the child had drifted off to sleep he thought the crisis was over. At nine-thirty he declared bedtime for Merry and Peter, who loudly protested that they didn't have a bedtime, that on weekends they could stay up forever if they wanted to.

Dan wasn't conned by them. He knew two sleepy children when he saw them, and fifteen minutes after their heads touched the pillow Merry and Peter were fast asleep.

But Butch was awake and being sick all over his sheets. Dan began to get alarmed. He'd blamed the first sickness on something Butch ate, but twice might mean it was something serious.

It was too late to call the druggist and not serious enough to alarm Betty June in Memphis. Dan washed Butch's face, changed the sheets and sat down beside the bed, pondering what to do. Janet. Her name suddenly popped into his mind.

He left the bedroom and went straight to the phone. She answered on the second ring.

"Hello." She sounded cool and professional. He felt better just hearing her voice.

"Janet?"

"Dan?"

"I'm sorry to call you so late."

"It's not late. And I'm glad you called. I've felt guilty about turning down your offer."

"There's no need. I understand . . . Janet?" He suddenly felt uncertain about what to say. Doctors were highly paid professionals, busy people. He didn't know of any of them who made house calls anymore. Taking advantage of friendships had never been his style, and yet Butch was his nephew.

"Dan, what's wrong?"

He breathed a sigh of relief. It was almost as if she had read his mind.

"Butch is sick . . ."

"I'll be right over."

She arrived within ten minutes. Dan was waiting at the front door.

As always, her first impact on him was staggering. The radiance of her skin, the richness of her hair, the beauty of her face almost took his breath away. Tonight was the same... until he saw the black bag. It was a sobering sight. Even when he'd visited her in her clinic and seen her in the white lab coat, he still hadn't had a clear vision of her as a doctor. But when she came through his door carrying the black medical bag, he was suddenly very much aware of Janet Hall as a doctor. His emotions warred within him: at the moment he needed her as a doctor, but he also needed her as a warm and sympathetic woman.

"Tell me about Butch, Dan." She was coolly, strictly professional.

"He vomited shortly after eight and again around nine. He doesn't appear to have a fever, but I thought twice in an hour's time was too much to be a simple upset stomach because of something he ate."

"Where is he?"

Dan led the way down the hall to one of his guest bedrooms. Butch looked tiny and fragile in the large cherry four-poster bed. Janet hesitated slightly in the doorway, looking from the sick child to his worried uncle. Dan went straight to the bed and hovered over his nephew, concern and fear etched in his face.

Never had keeping her professional distance been harder for Janet. Butch Mayhew had been her patient for three years, since he'd been born, and she had never had any trouble being his doctor. But tonight was different. She wanted to rush to the bedside and take both child and uncle into her arms, to soothe them with soft words and tender touches. *This is why doctors can't care for their own children during times of illness,* she thought.

The child was sick. Now was not the time for sentiment. Taking a deep breath she opened her bag and took out the things she needed—thermometer, stethoscope, blood-pressure cuff.

"Dan, will you sit over there in the chair so that I'll have more room to work?"

He obeyed her quiet command, settling into the rocking chair and watching as she ministered to his nephew. But he didn't watch quietly. Dan was not the type to sit by in silence when someone he loved was facing a crisis.

"Do you think it's something he ate, Janet?"

"Possibly. Did he complain of stomach cramps?"

"No. He said his stomach growled."

Janet smiled. "That's a typical child's way of describing a queasy stomach." She took the thermometer out of his mouth. "Temperature's normal." She put the pressure cuff on him.

Butch opened one drowsy eye and murmured sleepily, "That feels funny." Then he drifted back to sleep.

"Betty June will never forgive me if I let something happen to Butch."

Janet read the pressure before she answered him. "There's no need to panic, Dan. It's probably a simple stomach virus."

"Are you always this calm?"

She wasn't as calm as she appeared, but she was glad Dan couldn't see her turmoil. Distraught parents and guardians would not be served by panicked doctors, and neither would the patients. She trained her stethoscope on Butch's small chest and answered Dan. "Yes."

"I guess I should be glad."

She straightened up and looked at him. "I'm a doctor, Dan. This is my job."

"Then, Doc, what's your diagnosis?"

"Butch is a healthy three-year-old with a common childhood ailment—what most people describe as an upset stomach."

"What will we do about it?"

"We will hope that he doesn't vomit again. If that continues, however, we will use suppositories, which will be immediately effective in stopping the problem." She snapped her bag shut.

Dan had never been more aware of her career than at that moment. He was deeply grateful to her, and at the same time he was angry.

"You make it all sound so clinical."

"It is."

"No, it isn't." Dan left his chair and went to the bedside. "This child is my nephew, my flesh and blood."

Janet reached out and touched his arm in a gesture of compassion. "I know that, Dan. But I have to think of him objectively, otherwise my emotions might hamper my judgment."

Dan covered her hand with his. "Intellectually, I understand what you're saying...and I am truly grateful to you for coming here tonight."

"But?"

"What?"

"I sense reservations, Dan."

"Reservations, yes. And conflicting emotions." He squeezed her hand. "Ahh, Janet. Tonight I needed your skills, your medical knowledge. But I also needed... wanted..." He took his hand away. "Hell, I don't know what I wanted." In a gesture of frustration, he ran his hand through his hair. "I'm sorry, Doc. I stood you up, then dragged you out of your house and deprived you of your free evening—and now I'm lecturing like some depraved idiot."

She gave him a small smile. "I'm accustomed to distraught parents, Dan."

"But?" When she didn't immediately answer, he looked deeply into her eyes. "I hear reservations in your voice, too, Janet."

"What happens to us, Dan?"

He knew what she meant, and he wasn't sure he wanted it put into words. Instead of replying, he reached out and ran his fingers lightly down her cheek.

She shivered. "Don't."

His fingers hovered there, not leaving but not touching. "Why?"

"This..." She hesitated, searching for the right words. Then in a gesture of frustration, she windmilled her right hand in the air. "... whatever you want to call it—conflict, misunderstanding, lack of trust. You know what I'm talking about, Dan."

"Yes."

"It's always there between us."

"I don't want it to be."

"Neither do I."

They faced each other in the bedroom and it was almost as if the sleeping child had floated off the bed and positioned himself between them. They stood that way a while, separated by a chasm that had many names.

Dan was the first to bridge the gap. He reached out and swiftly pulled her into his arms. One hand braced her head and the other tucked her hips closer to his.

"Dan, we can't keep solving our problems this way."

"I know. But right now I don't want to think of another way." He lowered his head, and when his lips were only a fraction of an inch from hers he whispered, "I need you, Janet."

His need pulsed through him like vintage wine, heating his blood, warming his heart. Everything he was feeling communicated itself in his kiss.

Janet received him, took all his need and his turmoil and transformed it into an exquisite tenderness. Fires burned under the gentleness, but both of them kept the flames at bay. They were both raw and hurting, and they needed the healing balm of a lingering, tender joining.

Finally Dan lifted his head and gazed down into her eyes. "You always do that to me, Doc."

"What?" she whispered.

"Distract me."

She ran her hands over his face, caressing the high planes of his cheekbones and the sculpted wonder of his lips. "Do you think we could live a life of distraction?"

Her wistful question hung in the air for a moment. From the bed, Butch sighed in his sleep. Somewhere in the house the grandfather clock struck the hour. Eleven-thirty.

"If I had a magic wand, I'd stop time right now. I'd capture this moment in a time frame so that we could be this way forever. Just you and me. Two people holding each other."

"That's a beautiful thought, Coach."

His smile was both wise and sad. "Sometimes I wish I weren't an intelligent creature who knew better."

"So do I."

"It's getting late. You should be in bed."

Some of the old playfulness came back, and she smiled wickedly. "Your bed?"

Dan lifted one rakish eyebrow and then sobered. "If I ever get you there, Janet, I'll never let you go."

"I would never want to go, Dan."

"Perhaps we could shove our problems under the bed."

"They might make such a big hump that the mattress would be one-sided and we'd slide off onto the floor."

"Ahh, Doc... my beautiful Doc..." He ran his fingers through her hair. "We're not that far apart. I won't let us be."

She closed her eyes and fought her desire to close her medical bag forever, to shove it into a corner of a closet, climb into Dan Albany's bed and never look back. Instead, she did a sensible thing. "It's getting late."

"I've kept you up. I'm sorry."

"I'm glad I could be here for you." She pulled reluctantly away and reached for her bag. Smiling at him over her shoulder, she said, "Don't tell a soul that I made a house call."

"Seal my lips, Doc."

She moved back to him for a brief, hard kiss. And when it was over she felt almost as if she had told him goodbye. "I'll see you, Dan."

He took her elbow and escorted her out of the bedroom and down the hallway. "I wish I could drive you home. It's late."

"I'm used to being on my own, Dan. And although I am female, I'm perfectly capable of looking after myself." She didn't know why she'd said that, when a simple "thank-you" would have done. She guessed she felt some perverse desire to call attention to their problems. It was almost like having an open wound that wouldn't heal because it was constantly being poked and prodded. To make amends, she added, "Call me again if you need me. I can be here in ten minutes."

"If I need you..." His face was naked with longing. Janet leaned against the front door frame, and Dan propped one hand on the wall behind her. "I'll always need you, Janet."

He touched her lips in a kiss so filled with pent-up passion that she thought she would burn from the fire racing through his blood. When it was over they exchanged a long, deep look.

"Call me, Dan," she whispered. Then she backed swiftly through the door, turned and hurried to her car.

Sunday morning came in an ordinary way, with the sun rising in the east, melting away the veil of darkness that had shrouded the earth. Everywhere in Tupelo lights came on and people stirred from their beds.

In the Victorian house on Church Street, Harvey rose early, his ears pricked and his sap rising. He padded past the sleeping children and peered out the window. Across the way, that gorgeous poodle was sniffing the air as if she felt something great and wonderful had been let loose and she didn't want to miss it.

Harvey stretched leisurely, taking time to feel the vibrant glow of good health, and then he puffed out his chest in a show of male ego. Lifting his head, he sniffed. Something wonderful *was* in the air. And he knew precisely what it was.

Ordinarily he loved to go into Dan's bedroom and poke his nose under the covers, just to be absolutely sure his master didn't oversleep; but this morning he had more important things on his mind. Without waking a soul, he padded quietly through the house and through his doggie door. In the backyard he strutted and preened. Gwendolyn, that foxy lady next door, came to the fence and peered through. She whined. Harvey woofed softly.

And then they both began to dig. The hole was soon big enough for Gwendolyn to slip through. Once she was in his yard, Harvey took his time, courting her like the perfect Southern dog he was. A true lady like Gwendolyn came along once in a lifetime, and he had more sense than to spoil it with rash behavior.

She succumbed to his courtly manners, just as he knew she would, and soon they sought a lovers' retreat in the shelter of a big hydrangea bush that guarded Dan's back door.

Harvey decided that being in love was the best thing that had ever happened to him. With a curvaceous canine like Gwendolyn, he might even consider settling down. He was definitely going to have a little fling.

At his urging, Gwendolyn followed him to the gate and watched in admiration as he nosed aside the latch. The gate swung open, and together they headed down the street to great and wondrous adventures.

Dan didn't immediately discover that Harvey was missing. He had too much on his mind. He'd spent most of the night in a chair beside Butch's bed, watching and waiting. When he had finally decided the crisis was past and had gone to his own bed, his sleep had been restless and broken by frequent dreams.

Consequently when he awakened on Sunday morning he was tired and cranky, two feelings so foreign to him that he decided he was coming down with something serious.

All four children were out of bed by eight, as lively and bouncy as four rubber balls in a juggling act. By the time Betty June arrived to take them home, Dan was feeling frazzled and fractious.

His sister came into the house in her usual breezy manner, dispensing hugs and advice at the same time.

"Merry, I'm going to have to call you my little raspberry girl. Go in the bathroom, honey, and wash the jelly off your face.... Good land, Butch, you and Sam quit bouncing on Uncle Dan's sofa. My goodness. I have to put my feet up just a minute.'' She settled into the rocking chair beside Dan's fireplace.

Dan propped one elbow on the mantel and observed the chaos in his house. It was the first time in his life he'd ever considered that his sister's four children were rowdy. Was he getting old? he wondered.

"How was Memphis, Betty June?''

"Great. Ron was so carried away with the exhibit that he started working on a Rodin lecture as soon as we got back. How did it go here?''

"Butch was sick last night. Upset stomach.''

"He looks healthy enough now. One of them always has a stomachache or a runny nose or a stubbed toe.''

"I called his doctor. I didn't want to take any chances.''

Betty June leaned back in her chair and beamed at her brother. "Are you sure you called the doctor for Butch?''

"Not entirely.''

"Well, don't look so glum about it. In a romance, any excuse to see your lover will do.''

"It's not like that, Betty June.'' Dan gazed at his sister, but he was not seeing her. He was seeing a woman with dark red hair and bright brown eyes. "In fact, I don't know what it's like. Everything always seems to go wrong between us.''

His sister stood up and put her hands on her hips. "Dan, you've been a bachelor too long. I think you're scared to death of commitment.''

"Scared? I've never been scared of a thing in my entire life. I'd walk into a pit of snakes and not be scared.''

"I know it. But for some reason you're scared to walk down the aisle.''

"I've never found the right woman.'' Unconsciously his chin came up in a gesture of defiance. "When I find the right woman, *then* I'll walk down the aisle.''

"Well, now, let me see. Twenty years ago there was Sandra, who was just too flighty, and five years after that there was that horse-faced blonde with legs that reached from here to Arkansas . . . what was her name?"

"She wasn't horse-faced, and her name was Gretchen."

"Ahh, yes. Gretchen. I believe her failing was that she was a daddy's girl." Betty June ticked the women off on her fingers. "And then there was Maria . . . the one who talked too much. After her came Sylvia . . ."

"Stop." Laughing, Dan held up his hand. "Saying I'm scared just because I didn't marry any of them is stretching things a bit far. They were all seriously flawed."

"Humph." She turned to her children. "Merry, Peter, go get your things so we can go home." Then she faced her brother again. "I suppose you've found some serious failing in Dr. Janet Hall. Don't look so surprised. Your face is a dead giveaway. You look like a man caught with one foot in Heaven's gates and one on a banana boat sliding into hell."

"Banana peel."

"Whatever." She pinched his cheek. "You look a sight, Dan. Better call your doctor."

Merry and Peter came back with their overnight satchels, and Betty June gathered her children and started toward the door.

"Bye, Uncah Dan."

"Can we come back next week?"

"Can we see six moo-bees nex' time?"

All the children were talking at once. Betty June turned to wave at her brother. "Remember what I said, Dan."

Call your doctor. The phrase echoed in his mind after his sister had gone. In order to clear his head, he decided to go for a long walk. He got his leather jacket from the hall tree and crammed his baseball cap on his head.

Still standing in the hallway he called his dog. "Harvey. Come on, boy. Let's go for a walk."

When there was no answer he walked through the house, searching the rooms one by one. Then he checked the back-yard. The first thing he saw was the open back gate. The next thing he saw was the hole under the fence.

"Harvey, you old son of a gun." Dan was grinning when he said it. "Might as well take that walk without him."

The streets were Sunday-morning empty, and the air was clear and crisp in a way that happens only in January. Dan ambled down Church Street, not walking for exercise but meandering along to the jumbled tune that was playing in his head.

Without consciously planning it, he soon found himself standing at Janet's front door. He did the next natural thing: he knocked. She didn't come immediately to the door, so he knocked again. When she didn't answer that summons, he decided she was either at church or at the hospital on an emergency call.

He was just turning to leave when he heard his name being called.

"Dan!" Janet was across the street, waving.

He crossed over quickly. She was dressed in wool slacks and jacket, and her cheeks were pink from cold. Seeing her so unexpectedly made him feel almost shy. He gazed down at her as if he hadn't seen her in years. Finally she broke the silence.

"How's Butch?"

"He's fine. There were no more problems."

"That's good."

There was another awkward pause.

"I thought you would be in church," he said.

"I had to get out this morning. Somehow I couldn't bring myself to be cooped up inside with a crowd of people."

"Neither could I." They looked at each other for a long while, their eyes searching, their breaths making small cloud puffs in the air. "I went for a walk and I ended up at your front door."

"We always end up at each other's front doors. Don't we, Dan?"

"Yes. It must be significant."

"That's one of the things I'm trying to sort out this morning." She lifted her hand as if she would touch him, then slowly withdrew it.

"Have you come to any conclusions?"

"Yes."

"And?"

"I've come to the conclusion that there is no easy solution to our problem . . . there might even be no solution."

"I won't accept that." He reached for her hands. "No gloves? Doctor, you need somebody to take care of you." He blew on her cold hands, then rubbed them between his warm ones. Finally, he reached into his jacket pocket and pulled out a pair of fur-lined leather gloves. "Wear these, Doc."

"I'm just going across the street."

"Back home?"

"Yes."

"I'll escort you." Putting one arm around her waist and holding one of her cold hands in his, he led her back across the street. Standing in her parking lot, still holding on, he said, "Have you seen Harvey today?"

"No. I thought he was still at your house."

"So did I. But he's missing again."

"You don't sound too distraught."

"I'm not. I suspect he's courting. There's a big hole under the fence between my yard and the one next door, and the back gate is open."

"How does that add up to a courtship?"

"Didn't I tell you? Harvey seems to have taken a shine to the fancy big poodle next door. Gwendolyn."

Janet laughed. "Romance is so simple for dogs."

Dan looked wistful. "If I tried barking and wagging my tail, would you disappear with me?"

She considered all the possibilities of disappearing with Dan. The prospect made her cheeks burn. "I would probably take it as a symptom of mental disorder and recommend a good psychiatrist."

"What if I throw in sitting up and begging?"

She laughed. "In that case, I might invite you in for a cup of hot chocolate."

As they entered her condo she reflected on how easy it was to laugh with Dan. In that way he had added a rare dimension to her life. With Guy there had been a certain amount of passion and companionship, but never the easy laughter. It was something she couldn't dismiss without thought.

They hung their coats in the hall closet and went into the kitchen. Dan helped her measure cocoa and sugar and milk. When she started to zap it in the microwave, he stopped her.

"Let's do it the old-fashioned way." Digging around in the cabinets, he came up with a pan. He put the pan on the stove, poured the mixture in and turned on the gas. "It stays hot longer this way."

"It also takes longer to prepare."

"Some things are worth waiting for."

"Are they, Dan?"

They faced each other in the small kitchen. They weren't talking about hot chocolate anymore, and both of them knew it. Janet could feel the tension in his big body, see it in the tightened muscles, the hardened jawline, the heavy throbbing pulse at the side of his throat.

Her own hands were clenched, and she didn't know whether she was trying to keep from crying or shouting or from taking his hand and leading him into her bedroom. It would be so easy to assuage her pain with passion. It would be so easy to let their differences merge in a moment of sweet forgetfulness. It might even be easy to put little Randy Sanderford out of her mind with an interlude of ecstasy.

Tension climbed high in her chest and exploded. She whirled to the stove, grabbed an insulated glove and took the hot pan off. "Chocolate's ready," she said.

"I've lost my appetite."

"Well, I haven't." She jerked a teacup out of the cabinet and poured the steaming liquid. It sloshed over the side of the cup and spattered on her wrist. An angry red welt rose up.

"Dammit, Janet. You've burned yourself."

Still holding the hot pan, she faced him. "I'm a doctor. I can take care of it."

His jaw clenched. Stalking across the kitchen he got a dishcloth, wrapped it around the hot handle and lifted the pot from her hands. It clanked as he banged it back down onto the stove. Then he took Janet's arm and examined it.

All their differences seemed bound in that small red wound.

"Does it hurt?"

"Yes."

"I'll make it better." He lifted her wrist to his lips and kissed it.

"I'm afraid that's not the solution, Dan." She pulled her hand out of his grasp and walked through the kitchen and into her den. He followed her. While he watched she pulled ointment from her medical bag and opened the tube.

"Here. At least let me do that." He took the ointment from her, squeezed a small amount on her wrist and began to rub the wound. "This should never have happened, Janet. I'm sorry."

"I was careless. It's not your fault."

"In a way it is. I keep baiting you without really saying what's on my mind."

"What's on your mind, Dan?"

"You." Holding her hand, he gazed into her eyes. "I want you in a way that is totally selfish. I want your respect, your time, your passion, your body. I want you to be unconditionally mine."

"I don't think that's possible."

"I know it." Unconsciously he rubbed the small wound on her arm. "I keep hurting you."

"I'll get over it."

"I'm not talking about the burn."

"I know that, too, Dan. And I'm sure that in many ways I hurt you." She could see in his face that she was right, and the knowledge saddened her. It was time to stand back and assess their relationship. Quietly she pulled her hand out of his grasp. "Next week is going to be very busy for me."

"It will be busy for me, as well. The Eagles have two games, which means some long, hard practice sessions."

Janet knew the pain of parting she saw in his face was mirrored in her own.

"This is the best way, Dan. I think we both need some time to think."

"Perhaps you're right." He gazed at her a moment longer, then lifted his hand in a small salute. "I'll see you, Doc."

"Let me get your coat."

"There's no need for you to bother. I know the way out."

He walked out of the den and she heard his footsteps echo in the hall. The hall closet opened, then shut. There was a brief silence as he put on his coat, then she heard the front door open.

Something inside her snapped. She hurried to the hallway, calling, "Dan!" But it was too late. He had already gone.

She considered following after him, but rejected that notion. Then she thought of waiting until he reached his house and phoning him. But she discarded that idea, as well. He had said he wanted her respect, her time, her passion, and her body. He had said nothing about love.

There had been hints, plenty of them. But never once had either of them said, "I love you."

Janet studied her hallway—the polished floor, the soft wallpaper, the Waterford crystal vase, the silk flowers. It was a beautiful, peaceful setting. But it was meaningless without Dan Albany. In a sudden moment of epiphany, she realized that she loved him, that she had been in love with him from the beginning.

If love had been spoken, could they have worked through their differences? Perhaps. But she wasn't going to rush out now and try. She had asked for time, and she would take it.

Going to her desk she took out a legal pad. She sat down, took her pencil and divided the paper into two columns. She labeled one side "problems" and the other side "solutions," and then she began to work.

At the end of an hour she was smiling. She wasn't finished yet, but it was gratifying to know that her scientific, analytical mind could be used for love as well as for medicine.

After Dan left Janet's condo, he jogged and then ran toward home. He needed activity, hard activity. He had a strong hunch that he had just made a severe tactical error with Janet, and that he was very close to losing the entire game.

Once he got home, he hopped into his truck and went to the school where he taught. Taking his key, he let himself into the gymnasium. He worked with the weights until he was exhausted. Only then did he sit down on one of the benches to think.

He supposed the trouble with the relationship was that he had approached it as he would any game. He had expected the entire courtship to play by the rules. Too late, he had discovered that there were no rules. But was it too late?

He refused to believe that. He would figure out a solution, and when he did he'd go back on the field and win.

Feeling better, he got into his truck and went home. A quick check showed that Harvey had not come home. "You must be doing better than I am, old man," Dan muttered to himself.

He gathered an armful of firewood and built a big fire in his den. When it was crackling nicely, he sat down in a rocker. A faint scent of jasmine drifted to him. He reached onto the table and picked up Janet's scarf. Holding it to his face he inhaled her fragrance. Need struck him with such force he groaned.

"I'll win, Doc. I promise you that."

Chapter Ten

Monday morning Janet ordered the final battery of tests on Randy Sanderford. By the time she had finished her hospital rounds and reached the clinic, she was tense and already feeling exhausted.

Eleanor cornered her in her office. "You look like death, Janet."

"Thanks."

"I mean it. You've got to take more time off for yourself or you're going to be burned out in ten years."

"I can't take off right now, Eleanor."

"Then take up a hobby. Knitting."

Janet immediately thought of Dan. "Do you knit?" he had asked. It seemed so long ago. She smiled.

"See. Just the thought of it makes you feel better. You wait right there."

Eleanor disappeared and came back with needles, five skeins of yarn and an instruction book. She placed the whole lot on Janet's desk.

"Here. Take these. They've been in my car for a week. I meant to start a sweater for Ken, but I think you need it more than he does."

"I can't possibly take the yarn you're going to use for your husband's sweater. Besides, I don't know the first thing about knitting."

"It's easy. Just follow the instruction book." Eleanor started for the door.

"Eleanor, come back here. I didn't say I'd take this."

"I don't have all day to argue. You have patients waiting." Chuckling, she disappeared through the door.

Janet had a long day at the clinic, and afterward she returned to the hospital. The first thing she did was study the final brain scans on Randy Sanderford. What she saw made her sick. The tumor was malignant. Brain cancer. And she had to tell his parents.

She straightened her shoulders and started toward Randy's room. His parents would be waiting, just as they did at the end of every day, waiting for some sign of hope, some encouraging word, some assurance from their doctor that everything was going to be all right.

Room 355 was just ahead. Janet pushed open the door and went inside.

Late Monday evening, while the glow of the setting sun was still in the sky, Harvey returned to Church Street. Dan, just home from soccer practice, looked out the kitchen window and saw him prance through the back gate that had been left open for his return. Close behind him was Gwendolyn, looking smug and self-satisfied.

Dan filled Harvey's dish with dog food and went outside. He set the dish beside the back door and waited for Harvey's usual exuberant greeting. All he got was a gentlemanly wag of the tail.

"I guess you're pretty hungry after being gone for two days."

Harvey came up and sniffed the food and then went back to his shy lover. They had a brief communication in dog language, and then they both came forward to share the supper dish.

"Is this your new girlfriend, Harvey? Or is she your fiancée now?"

Harvey thumped his tail and grinned.

"I suppose it will be up to me to ask for her hand in marriage."

Harvey whined his agreement.

Chuckling, Dan fastened the back gate and went back inside. He couldn't wait to tell Janet.

He was halfway into his coat when he remembered that they were supposed to be taking time to think. Telling her about Harvey wouldn't count, of course. She'd want to hear news of him. After all, he was her dog, too.

"Who are you kidding, Coach?" He paced the hall, totally unaware of one jacket sleeve dragging along behind him. "You can't stay away from the woman. Admit it."

Suddenly the truth hit him: he was in love with Dr. Janet Hall. He stopped dead still in the middle of his hallway. A huge smile spread over his face.

"I'm in love with her." He was so pleased with the sound of the words that he tried them out again. "I love Dr. Janet Hall."

He hurried down the hall, and only when his sleeve got caught in the front door did he realize that his jacket was half on and half off. Shrugging into the other sleeve, he headed for his pickup truck.

Jubilation filled him as he drove along. By the time he got to her condo he was fairly singing with joy.

She didn't answer the doorbell until the fourth ring. If he hadn't seen her Porsche in the driveway he'd have thought she was not at home.

He knew she would be surprised to see him, and he thought she might even be upset; but when she opened the door she was quiet and reserved, even subdued.

"Dan." She stood almost uncertainly in the doorway, then she opened the door wider. "Come in."

His first instinct was to sweep her into his arms and say, "I love you." But on second thought he decided to take his time, to set the stage and pick the right moment. It was almost like setting up a soccer goal and waiting for the perfect time to kick the ball.

He stepped into her entry hall. "I know it's late, but I wanted to tell you the good news about Harvey."

It seemed to take a moment for Janet to focus her thoughts on Harvey. Then she gave him a small smile. "There's no need for you to stand in the hall. Come into my den. You can tell me while we sit in comfortable chairs."

He followed her into the den. As she turned to face him he noticed that she was extremely pale. She still wore high heels and a dark green wool suit that made her skin look like translucent ivory by contrast. Gone were the rose and gold tones of a Rubens painting.

She obviously hadn't been home long enough to change, and she was probably very tired. He'd tell her about Harvey, then make a real date to tell her that he loved her—a dinner date with candlelight and wine and roses.

He settled into the chair beside her fireplace and she sat on the sofa.

"Harvey came home today—with his girlfriend."

"The poodle."

"Yes. Gwendolyn. From the looks of things I believe I'm going to have to ask for her hand in marriage so Harvey can make an honest woman of her."

"That's good news. I'm glad to hear it." Her smile was somewhat shaky and so were her hands. She picked up two long needles and a skein of navy blue wool.

"Are you knitting?"

"I'm trying. Eleanor gave me the wool today. She even got me started on this sweater at lunch break." She held the unfinished sweater up for his inspection. Her lips trembled slightly.

"It looks great to me."

"It's not great. It's awful." A tear trickled down her cheek.

Dan bolted from his chair in alarm. Crossing the room, he knelt beside the sofa and patted her hand. "It takes a while to learn. Betty June took four months to knit her first sweater. You'll get the hang of it."

"No, I won't. Just look at that." She pulled up a section of knitting that faintly resembled a sleeve. "It will reach clear to Kansas and ba...ack." The tears began to rain down her cheeks in earnest.

"Hey, now." She made a high, keening sound of despair. Dan quickly sat on the sofa and pulled her into his arms, putting her head against his chest and smoothing her hair with his big hands. "There now, Doc. Don't cry, baby. It's not important. I don't care if you never pick up another knitting needle as long as you live."

She sobbed against his shirt. "I wanted...to do...it. Not just...for you. For me...to re-e-ela-a-ax."

He'd never seen Janet anything but composed. He guessed he had thought she wasn't even capable of tears. The thought shamed him. Being a doctor didn't make her any less human; it just made her more controlled.

"There, now, sweetheart. There now." He rocked her in his arms, soothing and stroking. But her sobs got harsher. Her shudders were hard against him, and he suddenly realized that she would never grieve so over failure to knit a sweater. "Tell me what's wrong, Doc."

"I'm tired . . . so tired."

"I know, sweetheart." He kissed the top of her hair. "Tell me about it."

"Oh, God, Dan." Janet lifted her tear-stained face. "He's going to die."

"Who?" When she was silent, he prodded gently. "Let me share this burden with you. Tell me, Janet."

"Randy Sanderford . . . I had to tell his parents tonight." She sniffed and took a deep, gulping breath. "He has a malignant brain tumor. Inoperable."

"I'm so sorry." He stroked her hair, her face, her neck. "I wish I could ease your pain."

Now that she had started talking about Randy, she seemed to gain strength and courage. Her voice became stronger as she talked. "He's so young, Dan. He said he wanted a car like Batman when he grew up. He'll never grow up." She paused.

"I'm listening, sweetheart."

"We can buy him a little time with chemotherapy . . . just a little time . . . a year, maybe two. . . . When I begin to think that science and medicine can cure every disease, when I get carried away with my own power, something like this happens to give me the right perspective." She lifted her head and looked at him. "It's so hard to be helpless in a situation like this. Randy and his parents came to me for help. I feel as if I've betrayed them."

"That's not true. And I'm sure they don't feel that way."

"No. They were very sweet . . . brokenhearted, but sweet."

"And you *have* given them something. You've given them hope." She sat quietly, waiting for him to continue, content to rest in the shelter of his arms. "Who knows what will happen in the next year or two? Perhaps a cure for cancer will be discovered. Or there might even be a miracle for Randy."

"Do you believe in miracles, Dan?"

"Yes, Janet. Do you?"

"I believe in science and knowledge...." Pausing, she stared into space. But she wasn't looking outward; she was looking inward. She was seeing the things in life that defied logic and reason: the flight of the bumblebee, the beaching of whales, the suicidal plunge into the sea of the lemmings. Life was filled with mysteries and miracles.

"To a certain extent, I do, Dan."

She leaned her head back against his chest. How good it felt to rest and be comforted! It was a luxury she hadn't had in many years.

Dan kissed the top of her head. "My mother had a wonderful cure for the blues."

"I can't think of one better than this."

"She used to run a tubful of hot water and pour in bubble bath. There was a special jar just for the occasion. When we were still small, she'd come in and scrub our backs and tell funny stories. After we got too big for that, she'd stand outside the door and yell through, 'Did you hear the one about old Mr. Pritckens. He started to hang flypaper strips on his front porch and his golden retriever got his tail stuck in the rosin. He like never to have gotten the dog loose. Said he thought he was going to have to hang old Sweetpea from the ceiling. Said he bet it was the biggest fly anybody ever caught.'"

"You do wonderful voices, Dan. Have you ever thought of going on stage?"

"I'd feel funny up there. I belong on a field somewhere, with a soccer ball between my feet."

She lifted her head and smiled at him. "Thank you, Dan, for . . . everything."

"You're welcome."

He held her in silence while the minutes ticked by. Finally he stood up and lifted her off the sofa.

"What are you doing?"

"I'm going to give you the complete blues cure."

She smiled. "Your mother's cure?"

"With variations."

He set her gently on her feet. "Don't move from this spot."

He left the room and she could hear his footsteps as he searched her small house. She heard doors opening and closing and finally the sound of water running. When he came back into the room he turned the lights down low and checked to be sure the draperies were closed. Then he came toward Janet, his face filled with love and tenderness.

With one hand he brushed her soft hair back from her face and with the other he unfastened the top button on her suit.

"I can do that, Dan."

"I want to take care of you, Janet."

He popped the second suit button open, and then the third and the fourth. She stood very still, luxuriating in the feeling of being pampered.

He slid the jacket from her shoulders, his hands skimming over her shoulders, sending heat waves through her silk blouse and warming her skin. He folded the jacket neatly then aimed it like a discus toward the sofa. It sailed through the air and landed on the cushions, still folded.

He smiled at her. "That's one of the small compensations of being a coach. You can do laundry in one room and deliver it to the closets in the next without ever taking a step.''

"Why is it that you can always make me smile?"

"Is that a smile I see? Can it be? Ahhh…I do believe it's a grin."

Chuckling, she turned and started toward the bathroom.

Dan put his hands on her shoulders and turned her back to face him. "Where are you going, Doc?"

"To the tub. That *is* a bubble bath I hear, isn't it?"

"Yes." His hands descended to the front of her blouse. "But this therapy has to be done in proper order to work." He opened the top button. Slipping one hand inside her blouse he began a gentle massage. "I'm going to undress you, and then I'm going to carry you to the tub. You'll sink under the water, with bubbles up to your neck, and I'll sit beside you and tell you funny stories."

While he talked he continued the massage. His words and the movements of his fingers were mesmerizing. Her neck began to feel limber and she let her head drop back. Closing her eyes, she gave herself up to the persuasive magic of Dan Albany.

"Afterward I'll light a fire and sit beside you on this rug. We'll drink wine and cuddle. You'll tell me your secrets and I'll tell you mine."

"It sounds wonderful."

"It's the healing power of togetherness."

He unfastened the second button on her blouse. Underneath he could see the delicate lace of her slip and the satiny sheen of her skin. Desire walked over him wearing storm-trooper boots, and a great shudder passed through his body. Not tonight. Tonight was a time for giving.

He tugged her blouse from her waistband and unfastened the rest of the buttons. The silk garment slid off her shoulders. They were the color of the rich country cream his grandmother used to skim off the top of the milk, and they were lightly dusted with gold freckles. He leaned down and kissed the freckles, one by one.

Janet put her hand in his hair, urging his head closer.

"Ahh, Dan. I'm so glad you came tonight."

"So am I." He kissed the pulse spot at the base of her neck, and then lifted his head. "We're going to be good together, Doc."

"Hmm."

He put his hands on her shoulders and slid his hands down the length of her arms, pushing the silk blouse aside. It fell into a heap at her feet. Dan stooped to pick it up, folded it and neatly tossed it onto the sofa with her suit jacket.

His eyes darkened to the color of a storm-tossed sea as he looked down at her. One hand traced the lacy top of her slip. Chill bumps popped out on her breasts.

"You are beautifully and wondrously made, Doc."

"Thank you."

He studied her with a reverence that trapped her breath in her throat. For one heady moment she thought he was going to lift her up and carry her into the bedroom. Instead he slowly knelt in front of her.

With the greatest of care he unfastened her skirt and pulled it down over her hips. Inch by inch he lowered the skirt until she was standing before him wearing only her slip.

Holding the skirt he stood up slowly, never taking his eyes off her.

"You look delicious, like a ripe peach."

She smiled. "It's the slip. Actually, that's the color. Peach."

"It's the woman."

He reached out and with his index finger traced the line of her body from breast to hip. "I envy that garment, the way it covers your body, clinging to your curves and settling into your hollows as if it belongs there."

A warmth blossomed in Janet, and she felt the sweet rush of heat throughout her body.

"Dan..."

"Shhh..." He put a finger on her lips.

Without taking his gaze off her, he tossed the skirt onto the growing pile of clothes.

"I want you, Janet. Make no mistake about that." He put his hands on her shoulders and eased her straps down. "But tonight I want to give you something that has nothing to do with passion and everything to do with love. I want to give you tenderness and compassion and understanding and humor and support. I want you to know without a doubt that I am your best friend, that you can count on me in all circumstances.... Do you trust me, Doc?"

"Yes."

"Then everything is going to be all right."

He caught her slip and pulled it over her head. She stood before him clad only in lace panties and a wisp of a bra. The muted lamplight gilded her skin so that she looked like a lush peach ripe for the tasting.

Dan lost his breath, and his heart climbed high in his chest, beating with eagle wings. He ran his fingertips lightly across the top of her breasts.

"'For thus merely touching you is enough.'" His voice was husky as he quoted Walt Whitman.

Reaching out with one hand, he unhooked her bra. She shrugged her shoulders and it slid to the floor. Keeping her eyes on his, she hooked her thumbs into the top of her bikinis and slid them down her legs.

Silently Dan crossed the small space that separated them. His eyes were bright with unspoken love as he lifted her in his arms and carried her into the bathroom.

The faucets were still running, not full force but in a steady stream, and bubbles filled the tub almost to the rim. He lowered her into the tub, then reached and turned off the taps. Water lapped over the edges of the tub and splashed on his shoes.

"You're getting wet, Dan."

"Not as wet as I will be." He pushed up the sleeves of his gray sweater and white shirt. "It's my philosophy that no bath worth taking is done alone."

She lifted her hair with both arms and leaned back. "This is sheer luxury."

"This is just the beginning." He turned and searched her vanity until he found two large tortoiseshell combs. "Allow me, Doc." He knelt beside the tub and secured the combs in her hair, then he leaned back to study the effect. Wispy curls escaped the combs and lay against her cheek and her neck. "Enchanting."

"Will I do to go to the symphony?" Entering into the spirit of fun, she postured for him, lifting an imaginary fan with one hand and making a big to-do of fanning.

"I can think of other places I'd rather take you."

They exchanged a long, deep look. Her cheeks flushed and her eyes grew bright.

"Dan, have I ever told you that I think you are a wonderful man?"

"I don't think so."

"Then it's long overdue. I think you are the most wonderful man I've ever known."

"Show me.

She put one soapy hand on his neck and pulled him forward. Her lips were warm and wet and slick and exquisitely tender. Steam rose around them, and the jasmine fragrance of her bubble bath perfumed the air.

When she released him, Dan sat back on his heels and gazed at her. "Doc, if you show me anymore, I'll be in that tub with you, clothes and all."

"I'd prefer you without clothes."

He wrestled with temptation. He was a passionate man, and it was only human to want to climb into a bubble bath with a gorgeous, sensuous woman. But tonight was his gift to Janet. He wouldn't let passion interfere.

His smile was somewhat wistful as he picked up a washcloth and began to lather it with soap.

"Next time, we share the bath, Doc. That's a promise.... Now, turn that beautiful back to me and I'll show you all the therapeutic techniques of a soccer coach."

While Dan massaged her back, he talked. "Did I ever tell you about Tolbert Simmons?"

"No."

"He was my grandfather's age, a spry old man, even in his seventies." He cast aside the cloth and began to massage with his hands. As he talked he could feel the tension easing out of her. "Folks called him the man who once died."

"Why?"

"That was back in the days before embalming. Old Tolbert died and was decked out in his casket. Mourners were passing by, crying and telling all the good things they knew about him. When Minnie Crimpton passed by, she leaned down and kissed him on the lips. Old Tolbert kissed her back. After all the celebrating was over, folks asked him what had happened. He said he'd always been sweet on Minnie, and he guessed he had to die to get her to kiss him."

Janet chuckled. "You made that up."

"Scout's honor. I did not." He sat back on his heels and watched her laugh. "I never thought a woman's laughter would be the sweetest music in the world."

"You say beautiful things."

"I'll always say beautiful things . . . for you." He reached into the water and caught one of her hands. Lifting it to his lips, he kissed her palm. "And now, m'lady, I'll leave you to your bath."

She touched her hand to his face. "Don't go," she whispered.

"I'm not leaving, sweetheart. I'm going to light your fire."

"You've already lit my fire." Her smile was wicked.

"And you've lit mine. . . . That calls for a celebration, don't you think?"

"Yes."

He kissed her knuckles and lowered her hand back into the water. "Finish your bath, love. I'll be right back."

Janet sank back into the water, smiling. He left the bathroom and she could hear him moving about her house. Knowing that he was there made her feel peaceful and safe, as if she were a storm-tossed bird that had come unexpectedly upon a huge, sheltering rock.

She lingered in the tub and soon he was back, carrying her pink terry-cloth robe. He hung the robe on the bathroom hook and smiled down at her.

"All finished, Doc?"

"Is this 'Twenty Questions'?"

"No. Only two."

"The first is whether I am finished with the bath. What's the second?"

"Who's the most wonderful man you know?"

She laughed. "Egotist."

Still laughing, she took his hand and stepped from the tub, her body slick and shining with bubbles. He wrapped her in a thick, fluffy towel and pulled her into his arms.

"You'll get wet, Coach."

"This is a new technique for drying. I call it press-and-dry."

He hugged her so close she could feel the steady throbbing of his heart. She placed her head over that reassuring sound and rested there, sighing.

"Thank you, Dan."

"I'm glad I was here for you." He stepped back and looked down at her. "I plan always to be here for you."

"Dan..."

"Shh..." He pressed a light kiss on her lips. "Tonight we're going to cuddle beside the fire and drink wine and relax. I'm going to wave my magic wand and banish all thoughts that aren't cheerful and pleasant."

She grinned at him. "Show me your magic wand."

"If I show you my magic wand, you're liable to forget yourself and tarnish my reputation beyond repair."

"And then I suppose I'd have to make an honest man of you by marrying you."

"Exactly. And we'll have no shotgun weddings, madame." He took the edges of the towel and gave her back a brisk massage and helped her into her pink terry-cloth robe.

Scooping her into his arms, he smiled down at her. "You look like pink cotton candy in that robe. I think I'll eat you up, a little bit at a time."

He growled playfully and nuzzled her neck. Her laughter echoed through the house as he carried her into the den. The room was cozy, filled with muted lamplight and the glow from the fireplace. Dan had turned on the gas, and the imitation logs were casting welcoming flame shadows over the white rug. Two crystal goblets filled with burgundy wine sparkled on a silver tray beside the fire.

Dan sat on the rug and arranged Janet on his lap.

"The head belongs here." He gently pressed her head back against his shoulder so that her cheek rested against his warm gray sweater. "And the legs here." He tucked her robe around her bare legs and made sure she was sitting solidly on his blue-jean-clad thighs. "Comfortable?"

"Enormously... The fire feels good. I haven't had time to light the gas all winter."

"Fires are always cozier when they are shared." He reached to the tray and picked up a crystal goblet. Holding it to her lips, he said softly, "Drink, sweetheart."

She took a small sip, then he raised the glass to his own mouth. He placed his lips over the precise spot hers had touched and took a long drink.

"It's sweeter having touched your lips."

He offered her the glass once more. She covered his hand with hers while she drank.

Outside a benevolent rain had begun to fall, sweeping quietly through the night, nourishing the earth and sounding its hypnotic music against the windowpanes. Lulled by the melody of the rain and the warmth of the fire, Janet closed her eyes, sighing.

Dan smiled and placed the empty glass on the silver tray.

Without lifting her head or opening her eyes, Janet spoke to him. "Dan?"

He caressed her hair. "Hmm?"

"Why are you doing this?"

"Friendship."

"That's all?" She opened her eyes to look at him.

He had meant to choose a different time to tell her, a time when she was strong and composed. She was hurting now, and vulnerable. He didn't want to take advantage of that. And yet...the time seemed right.

He looked deep into her eyes. "Because I love you, Janet."

Her cheeks flushed and her eyes became brighter. "What about your sweet, old-fashioned woman?"

"It's a funny thing about dreams. I've had that vision before me for years, and all along I was merely biding my time until the right woman came along." He traced the curve of her cheek with his finger. "You're that right woman, Janet. It took me a long time to figure it out, but you're the only woman I want, the only woman I need, the only woman I'll ever love."

"Would you be terribly surprised if I told you that I love you, too?"

"Not terribly."

They laughed together.

"Who could not love a man with your supreme self-confidence?"

"You used to call it arrogance."

"I used to call you a lot of things. Unsuitable, for one." She brushed one hand tenderly over his chest, reveling in the feel of his hard muscles beneath the soft gray sweater. "It was my way of protecting myself." Her hand played over his chin. "We have a lot to talk about, a lot of kinks to work out."

"We will. But not tonight. Tonight there will be nothing between us except love, no talk about the future, no talk about the past, no hurts, no problems. It's just you and me, Janet."

In one swift motion he rolled over so that she was lying on the white rug, her hair fanned out like flame on snow. He stretched out beside her and propped himself on his elbow so he could look into her face.

"Don't leave me, Dan. I don't want you to leave me tonight."

"I won't leave you, sweetheart. Not now, not ever."

He took her into his arms and began to kiss her. His lips touched her brow, her eyelids, her cheeks, her chin and finally her mouth. He understood her need. He understood that while she loved, she was also hurting. Little Randy Sanderford was still a raw and gaping wound.

With his kisses he absolved all her anguish, took on all her pain, transforming it into a distant aching regret that she could live with. He was balm to her soul. He was healer, protector and friend. He was love.

Chapter Eleven

They stayed beside the firelight a while longer, sharing the last glass of wine, sharing a tender kiss or two and holding each other close. At last Janet couldn't stifle a yawn.

"Bedtime, Doc."

He lifted her into his arms and made his way to her bedroom.

"Dan, do you plan to carry me around this way the rest of our lives?"

"Yes. It builds muscles and it's a lot more fun than lifting weights."

He swiftly crossed the room and lowered her to the bed. Lying there against the white comforter, she looked like a fallen rose petal. He traced her lips with his fingers.

"I'm going to sleep with you, Janet." When she started to say something, he put his finger over her lips. "Hush, love. Tonight I'm going to be a man of honor and iron control. I'm going to hold you in my arms all night long . . . merely hold you.''

He rose from the bed, and still looking down at her he unbuckled his belt and pulled it from his pants. The belt made a small thud as it hit the carpet. He bent down and untied his jogging shoes and kicked them aside. Then he stripped the gray sweater over his head and unbuttoned his white shirt.

The faintest ray of light shone through the window, the pale glow of a winter moon making its presence known after the rain. The fingers of light caressed Dan's bare chest, gilding his muscles and highlighting the sprinkling of dark hair on his chest.

''You are beautiful, Dan.''

He gazed down at her for the longest while, drinking deeply of her beauty. ''So are you.''

She lifted her hand to him. ''Come.''

She turned the covers back and he climbed into bed beside her. Taking her into his arms, he fitted her, spoon-fashion, against his body. Her fragrant hair brushed against his cheek.

''Comfortable, love?''

She sighed. ''You're better than a down quilt.''

''You're not too hot with that robe on?''

''You might as well know my awful secret: I get so cold in winter I sometimes sleep in wool socks.''

''I'm partial to women in wool socks.''

She pressed closer to him, reveling in the solid feel of his body, taking immense comfort from his reassuring presence and finding great joy in his unselfish love.

'' 'Night, Coach.''

''Good night, Doc.''

* * *

When Janet awakened the next morning, she thought Dan had gone. There was an indentation in the pillow where his head had been, and his clothes were no longer lying on the floor.

She yawned and stretched. She felt good, refreshed, revitalized. She sat up and was just swinging her feet over the side of the bed when Dan entered the bedroom, carrying a silver tray laden with food.

"Good morning, Doc. Sleep well?"

"Dan! I thought you had gone."

"What? Leave before my good-morning kiss. Never."

He sat on the edge of the bed, tray propped on his knees, and leaned over to kiss her. He tasted of strawberry jam.

Laughing, she leaned back against the pillows. "Been in the jam pot, have you?"

"I see it will be impossible to keep any secrets from you."

"Don't even try." She put her hands behind his neck and drew him forward for another kiss. "Mmm, I like strawberries in the morning."

"I come in other flavors, too. Grape, raspberry, orange, cherry, kumquat."

"Kumquat?"

"Just checking to see if you were paying attention."

She suddenly sat upright. "You'll be late for school."

"I've called for a substitute. I plan to devote the entire day to you."

She was thoughtful a moment. The man sitting on her bed had given unselfishly of himself; he had sacrificed time and passion to help her make it through a bad night. And now he was taking time away from his job just to be with her. A man like Dan Albany was a precious gift, and one she wasn't about to throw away.

"Thank you, Dan." Smiling, she reached for the bedside phone and dialed. Dan could hear a distant ringing, and then Janet began to speak. "Eleanor, this is Janet. Would you please reschedule my checkups and arrange for Dr. Lawrence to see my sick patients?... What? No, I'm not sick." She winked at Dan. "I'm staying home to knit."

After she had hung up, she and Dan burst into laughter.

"Doc, we're going to have a wonderful life together."

"Coach, is that a proposal?"

"No, but this is." Setting the tray on the bedside table, he knelt beside the bed and took her hand. "Janet, will you marry me?"

"Is this a multiple-choice test?"

"No. One choice."

She teased him by appearing to be deep in thought over her answer. He wiped imaginary sweat from his brow. Finally, she smiled.

"Yes, Dan. Oh, yes."

They reached for each other at the same time. Somewhere halfway between the bed and the floor, they met. Janet threw her arms around his neck, he tugged, and they both ended up on the floor, arms and legs tangled, kissing as if they would never stop.

"Hmm, you're better than strawberry," she murmured.

"And you're better than cotton candy."

Their lips joined again, and there was great hunger in the kiss. Dan rolled to his side, holding her tightly against his chest with one arm, and parting her robe with the other. His hand roamed over her bare legs until he found the spot he sought.

She sucked in her breath, and her heart thudded hard against her ribs. "Dan... please."

"A little magic before breakfast." He leaned back to watch her face. It held passion and was bright with pleasure.

"Ahh, love..." she murmured.

"Yes...it's love." He pulled her hard against his chest and buried his face in her hair. "Ahh, Janet. I love you so!"

She pressed her face into the warm hollow of his neck and softly kissed the pulse spot there. "And I love you."

"Will you want children, Janet?" He leaned back and looked into her face as he asked the question.

She loved him for that, for she knew how important children were to him.

"Yes. We'll have children, Dan. As many as I can, and if that's not enough we'll adopt."

He kissed the tip of her nose. "I neither expect nor want you to give up your career."

"I know that, but I'm glad you said it." She brushed his tousled hair back from his forehead. "I can have career and marriage and a family. It will take some adjustment. I'll have to rearrange my work schedule, perhaps get a partner or two, maybe even reduce my practice to part-time." She gazed at him with all the wonder of love in her eyes. "I want to make this work, Dan."

"So do I, Janet." He glanced around her bedroom. "I'll live here if you want. Or we can get another place, slightly bigger, but one suitable to your tastes."

"I've grown rather fond of that big, old house on Church Street."

His smile was bright enough to light all of Tupelo. "You mean that beautiful Victorian mansion so lovingly restored by the famous soccer coach?"

"That's it. The one that has room for Harvey and six kids in the backyard."

"Harvey and *Gwendolyn* and six kids and five puppies."

Laughing, they sat up and Dan lifted the tray off the bedside table. He set it on the floor between them and they began to eat the breakfast he had prepared.

Janet eyed the bacon and eggs. "I know this wasn't in my refrigerator."

"While you slept, I went to my house to get them."

"My love, this kind of food is okay on occasion, but I have to warn you that I'm a really tough doctor when it comes to proper diet. I'm planning to throw out your bacon, hot dogs and cream-filled cupcakes, and substitute wheat bran, yogurt and fresh fruit."

He grinned at her. "I'll try to eat just what my doctor orders, but I'm not making any rash promises."

"I didn't think you would."

As they finished their breakfast, they made plans for their future together, starting with a Valentine's Day wedding. Then Janet dressed and they went together to Dan's house on Church Street.

Harvey and Gwendolyn, who had entered the house through the doggie door, greeted them in the hallway with wagging tails.

"So this is your lady love." Janet bent over and patted Gwendolyn's head. "I know just how you feel, my dear."

Dan chuckled. "Not quite. I'm afraid Harvey hasn't been as restrained with his passion as I have."

Janet looked at him in mock outrage. "Careful how you tarnish a lady's reputation. See how insulted Gwendolyn looks."

"Not nearly as insulted as her owner, I'll bet. I think it's time to pay that dear lady a call."

Gwendolyn's owner was Miss Fannie Mae Small, and she was, indeed, outraged about Gwendolyn's fall from virtue.

Her pouty red mouth trembled and her fat yellow curls twitched as she shook her head angrily.

"My Gwendolyn is a dog of impeccable lineage. You mean to tell me she has spent the last two days in the company of that horrible unpedigreed *creature* you keep in your backyard?"

"I'm afraid so." Dan winked at Janet. "It appears to me the damage has already been done."

"You mean . . ." Fannie Mae covered her mouth with her hands and stifled a scream of horror. "Oh, my poor baby, my poor innocent b-a-a-be-e-e-e." She uncovered her mouth and glared at Dan. "Where is she? Where is my poor lamb?"

"She's at my house, with Harvey."

"She's still with him! Oh, dear. She'll never be the same."

"They seem quite taken with each other," Dan said.

"My Gwendolyn has better taste!"

"Apparently not."

Fannie Mae wrung her hands. "Oh, dear. What will I do? I did so want her to remain pure until I could have her fixed." She glared at Dan with malevolent little eyes. "She was going to be a great show dog, you know."

"Perhaps after the puppies are born . . ."

"Puppies!"

"It looks that way to me." He put his arm around Janet and stepped closer to Fannie Mae. "What my fiancée and I would like to do is buy Gwendolyn."

"You want me to sell my precious lamb?"

"Look at it as giving her hand in marriage. She would be right next door so you could see her any time you liked. And we would take very good care of her and the puppies. In the meantime, you could get another poodle and raise it to be a show dog."

"Well..." Her curls bobbed as she tossed her head this way and that, apparently in an agony of thought. Finally she said, "You may have her on one condition."

"What's that?"

"That your dog marry her. I'm not talking about some little puny backyard affair with a bogus preacher mumbling a few words: I'm talking about a real wedding."

Dan and Janet stared at each other, and then they began to grin.

"Are you thinking what I'm thinking, Doc?"

"A double wedding?"

"Why not?"

"Why not, indeed."

They both burst into laughter.

Janet and Dan's wedding day was clear and beautiful, with the sun trying to prove to the world that it was May instead of February. It gilded the steeple of the Episcopal church and shone benignly on the heads of the wedding guests as they assembled for the marriage ceremony.

Betty June and Ron came with their four children, all scrubbed and slicked up and shining, except for little Butch, who had found a black crayon in the back seat of the car and had painted himself a grand mustache, unbeknownst to either parent. As he passed down the center aisle he waggled his mustache at old Mr. Jeddidiah Rakestraw, sitting in the fourth pew. The old man slapped his thigh and chuckled.

Leaning over, he whispered to Michelle Leonard, "It's a sight what children will do."

She nodded her agreement.

In the pew in front of Mr. Jed, Eleanor turned around to wink at him.

Beside her, Billie Jean Haskins, who was prouder than a peacock to be invited to the wedding, adjusted her hat that she had bought especially for the occasion. It was bright purple with the most gorgeous peacock feather she had ever seen sitting right there on the brim, as cocky as you please. Hats always made a woman feel good. And it was perfect for the occasion. That nice receptionist of Dr. Hall's had told her so. What was her name? She was getting terrible about remembering names. Jane? Jill? Julie? Julie! That was it.

The organ music swelled and there was a rustle at the back of the church. Billie Jean broke off her musings to turn around and look. What she saw made her catch her breath. Dr. Hall was the most beautiful bride she had ever seen.

Janet began to walk slowly down the aisle, holding onto the arm of a very good-looking young man. Her brother, somebody had said. Wasn't he just the cutest thing who ever wore pants?

Then Dan took Janet's hand and the ceremony began. Billie Jean thought it was just about the grandest wedding she'd ever seen. A tear rolled down her cheek at the beauty of it all.

When the groom kissed the bride, Billie Jean bawled in earnest. It was a darned good thing she had bought a lace-edged handkerchief for the occasion. She sniffed into the hankie and leaned back to watch the groom escort his bride up the aisle and out of the church. She hoped they had chocolate cake at the reception. She'd been so excited about the wedding she hadn't eaten much breakfast, and chocolate was her favorite kind.

She was still dreaming of chocolate when the organ started up again. What was happening? she wondered. That was the Bridal March. She heard a commotion at the back of the church, and had to crane her neck to see over the crowd.

Fannie Mae Small appeared, mincing down the aisle in a goshawful pair of red high heels, looking as if she might topple over at any minute. Behind her trotted two dogs.

"My gosh. It's Harvey," Billie Jean said aloud. Two women in the next row turned around to shush her.

Harvey was now even with Billie Jean's pew. He wore a bow tie, and the big poodle next to him was wearing an honest-to-goodness veil. As the crowd murmured its astonishment, they walked straight to the front of the church and the minister started up another marriage ceremony.

The dog ceremony was brief, which was a blessing, because any fool could see that the bride was pregnant and in no condition to be standing around on her feet all day.

When it was over, and all the newlyweds had marched back down the aisle, Billie Jean was the first to head for the fellowship hall. She couldn't wait to see if the dogs had their own wedding cake. However would they cut it?

Dan carried his bride over the threshold.

After the ceremony they had flown straight to New York because Dan had said he needed an intensive course in culture in order to keep up with his new wife. She had booked tickets to at least three Broadway plays, and heaven only knew how many concerts.

But for now they had a spacious suite at the Plaza, and they had each other. Inside the room, he kicked the door shut and set his bride on her feet.

"How long has it been since I kissed you, Mrs. Albany?"

"Too long."

"Then we must remedy that."

And he did.

The kiss led to other things. Passion bloomed bright and hot and Dan, his lips still clinging to hers, began to back his wife toward the bed.

"Doc, I've waited so long to have you."

"Only a few weeks, Dan."

"It seems like forever."

He kept her close with one hand pressed against her hips, and with his other he began to unbutton her suit. It was a tight-fitting blue wool, with brass buttons from neck to waist and a flirty peplum over the hips. She wore it without a blouse, only a single strand of pearls, Dan's gift to her.

She smiled. "You're getting good at that."

"Practice makes perfect." He slid the jacket from her shoulders and tossed it onto a chair. "And I intend to have lots of practice."

"I would prescribe that for a good, healthy marriage."

"I always do what my doctor orders." He unhooked her skirt and slid it down her legs. What he saw made him drop the skirt heedlessly to the floor.

Janet was wearing a black lace teddy, so sheer he could see the ivory sheen of her body and the dark rose of her nipples. He ran his hand down the length of her, starting at her breasts and ending at the top of her thighs.

"You make me explode with love." Lifting one of her hands, he planted a tender kiss in the palm. "I plan to spend the rest of my life showing you how happy I am that you're mine."

Slowly she unbuttoned his shirt and pushed it aside. Lowering her head, she kissed him in the valley right over his heart. "Show me now." Her voice was husky.

Dan slipped out of the rest of his clothes and lowered her to the bed. His eyes worshiped her, his hands cherished her.

She arched to his fingers, crying out his name.

He stripped aside the last thing that separated them—the wispy black teddy—then raised himself on his knees to gaze down at her. She lay across the sheets, the neon lights of the city gilding her body. A slash of blue crossed her breasts, highlighting their hardened peaks and shading her skin the color of Easter eggs at springtime. Gold lights teased her navel and the downy skin of her stomach, and purple shaded her thighs.

"You're all the colors of the rainbow . . . and I love them all." He bent over her and began to kiss his way down her body, starting with the neon blue. She circled her arms around his neck and murmured sweet words to him. When he got to the gold she was moaning, and by the time he reached the purple she was writhing.

"Easy, love . . . we have forever."

"Now, Dan . . . oh, please."

He lifted himself and covered her body with his. In the time-honored way, he made her his own. Her warmth surrounded him and ecstasy filled his soul. The muscles in his arms quivered as he held himself in check, glorying in the wonder of being joined with this woman.

He lowered his mouth to hers, kissing with a heart-searing passion and a heartwarming thanksgiving. Their bodies moved in unison, seeking a greater joining.

Suddenly Dan lifted his head. "Doc?"

"I didn't tell you, Dan," she whispered. "You're my first."

"Ahh, Doc." He gathered her close and buried his face in her hair. " 'Give me the splendid silent sun with all his beams full-dazzling,' but even he would pale compared to you." He kissed her hair, her neck, her eyes. "You've given me a gift beyond compare. To know that you belong to me and me alone makes my heart soar."

"In some ways, I guess I'm old-fashioned."

"You never told me."

"You never asked." She clasped her hands around his neck and arched her hips against his. "Are we going to talk, Coach, or what?"

Dan thrust deeply, storming her citadel and making her his own.

"Or what," he whispered.

Epilogue

It was Janet's first delivery.

She bent over the basket of puppies on the hearth and smiled. "Six of them." Gently she lifted one and held it out for Mr. Jed's inspection. "Look at those floppy ears. Harvey has left his mark on all of them."

Mr. Jed leaned back in the rocking chair, chuckling. "Looks like somebody else has left his mark."

Janet lowered the puppy back to the basket and the doting attention of Gwendolyn. Smiling, she patted her rounded stomach. "That's why I invited you for tea. I wanted you to be the first to know."

Mr. Jed studied the big, high-ceilinged room with its comfortable mixture of classy Waterford crystal and Saturday-morning-auction memorabilia. "This big house needs children. And so do you and Dan. There's nothing like a child to make a man's life complete." There was a wistful, faraway look in his eye.

Janet rose from the hearth and went to his chair. Bending down, she put her arms around his shoulders. "You miss her, don't you?"

"Yes. It's been a while. But of course a parent can't be selfish. I raised Molly to be independent and, by George, that's exactly what she is."

"Where is she now?"

"Off in Paris somewhere—naked as a jaybird, I'll vow." Mr. Jed chuckled. "She's an artist's model." He laughed again with genuine glee. "I'll vow it's just an excuse to shock folks. Molly always was fond of shocking folks."

"I'd love to meet her." Janet moved to her own chair, the rocker that she'd grown to love.

"You will. And pretty soon, if I have my guess." Mr. Jed reached into his pocket and pulled out a letter. "Here. Read this." He handed it to Janet. "Carbon copy." The letter said:

Dear Molly,
I've taken quite a fancy to a wonderful woman by the name of Glory Ethel. Met her through the lonely-hearts column. If you want to meet your future stepmother before the wedding, you'd better hurry on home 'cause I'm getting too old to wait much longer.

Janet lowered the letter. "You're getting married, Mr. Jed?"

"Well, not till I meet Glory Ethel myself, of course. But I can tell you one thing: if she's half as nice in person as she is on the phone you can get set for a wedding that will give folks in Tupelo something to talk about."

Janet laughed. "They're still talking about Harvey's wedding."

"Let 'em talk. It's good exercise."

Mr. Jed stayed a while longer, enjoying the tea and company, then Janet drove him back to his condo. By the time she got back to the big house on Church Street, Dan was home from soccer practice.

He met his wife at the door.

"It's been too long since I kissed you, Mrs. Albany."

"Only since this morning."

"Like I said, too long." He pulled her into his arms for a thorough kiss. Then he walked to the hall table and picked up a package tied with pink and blue ribbons. "A gift for you."

Janet untied the ribbons and tore aside the paper. Inside the box was the tiniest baseball cap she had ever seen. She lifted the little cap from the box and smiled.

"They had a little baseball glove, too, but I didn't know whether to get pink or blue."

"You're working mighty fast, Coach. The baby's not even here yet and already you have her playing first base."

"That's what I am. A fast worker... Come here, Doc." He pulled her into his arms and began to nuzzle her neck.

"Are you gloating just because I came home from the honeymoon pregnant?" She kissed his ear. "It takes two, you know."

Grinning, he lifted her into his arms and began to stroll down the hall. "How well I know, Doc. How well I know."

When he reached the master bedroom, he carried her inside and kicked the door shut behind them.

* * * * *

Catch up on the characters you met in
HARVEY'S MISSING during July 1990—a month
for fireworks!—in the delightful Silhouette Romance
VENUS de MOLLY by Peggy Webb.

Silhouette ❀ *Romance*®

COMING NEXT MONTH

#718 SECOND TIME LUCKY—Victoria Glenn
A Diamond Jubilee Book!
Ailing Aunt Lizbeth glowed with health after Miles Crane kissed her man-shy goddaughter Lara MacEuan. If Miles had his way, his frail aunt would be on a rapid road to recovery!

#719 THE NESTING INSTINCT—Elizabeth August
Zeke Wilson's cynical view of love had him propose a marriage of convenience to Meg Delany. Could his in-name-only bride conceal her longing for a marriage of love?

#720 MOUNTAIN LAUREL—Donna Clayton
Laurel Morgan went to the mountains for rest and relaxation... but Ranger Michael Walker knew fair game when he saw it! The hunt was on, but who was chasing whom?

#721 SASSAFRAS STREET—Susan Kalmes
Callie Baker was furious when the man who outbid her at an antique auction turned out to be Nick Logan, her new boss. Nick, on the other hand, was thrilled....

#722 IN THE FAMILY WAY—Melodie Adams
Fiercely independent divorcée Sarah Jordan was quite in the family way—and had no plans for marriage. But smitten Steven Carlisle had plans of his own—to change her mind!

#723 THAT SOUTHERN TOUCH—Stella Bagwell
Workaholic Whitney Drake ran from her fast-paced New York life to the Louisiana bayou—and right into the arms of Caleb Jones. But could his loving touch convince her to stay forever?

AVAILABLE THIS MONTH:

SILHOUETTE DESIRE™
presents
AUNT EUGENIA'S TREASURES
by CELESTE HAMILTON

Liz, Cassandra and Maggie are the honored recipients of Aunt Eugenia's heirloom jewels...but Eugenia knows the real prizes are the young women themselves. Read about Aunt Eugenia's quest to find them everlasting love. Each book shines on its own, but together, they're priceless!

Available in December:
THE DIAMOND'S SPARKLE (SD #537)

Altruistic Liz Patterson wants nothing to do with Nathan Hollister, but as the fast-lane PR man tells Liz, love is something he's willing to take *very* slowly.

Available in February:
RUBY FIRE (SD #549)

Impulsive Cassandra Martin returns from her travels... ready to rekindle the flame with the man she never forgot, Daniel O'Grady.

Available in April:
THE HIDDEN PEARL (SD #561)

Cautious Maggie O'Grady comes out of her shell...and glows in the precious warmth of love when brazen Jonah Pendleton moves in next door.

SD-AET-1R

A BIG SISTER
can take her places

She likes that. Her Mom does too.

BIG BROTHERS/BIG SISTERS AND HARLEQUIN

Harlequin is proud to announce its official sponsorship of Big Brothers/Big Sisters of America. Look for this poster in your local Big Brothers/Big Sisters agency or call them to get one in your favorite bookstore. Love is all about sharing.

BB/BS-1A

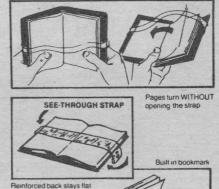

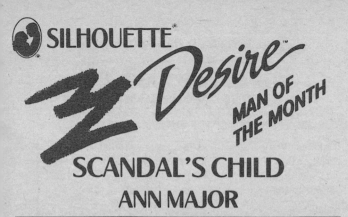

SILHOUETTE Desire

MAN OF THE MONTH

SCANDAL'S CHILD
ANN MAJOR

When passion and fate intertwine...

Garret Cagan and Noelle Martin had grown up together in the mysterious bayous of Louisiana. Fate had wrenched them apart, but now Noelle had returned. Garret was determined to resist her sensual allure, but he hadn't reckoned on his desire for the beautiful scandal's child.

Don't miss SCANDAL'S CHILD by Ann Major, Book Five in the Children of Destiny Series, available now at your favorite retail outlet.

Silhouette Romances

DIAMOND JUBILEE CELEBRATION!

It's Silhouette Books' tenth anniversary, and what better way to celebrate than to toast *you*, our readers, for making it all possible. Each month in 1990, we'll present you with a DIAMOND JUBILEE Silhouette Romance written by an all-time favorite author!

Welcome the new year with *Ethan*—a LONG, TALL TEXANS book by Diana Palmer. February brings Brittany Young's *The Ambassador's Daughter*. Look for *Never on Sundae* by Rita Rainville in March, and in April you'll find *Harvey's Missing* by Peggy Webb. Victoria Glenn, Lucy Gordon, Annette Broadrick, Dixie Browning and many more have special gifts of love waiting for you with their DIAMOND JUBILEE Romances.

Be sure to look for the distinctive DIAMOND JUBILEE emblem, and share in Silhouette's celebration. Saying thanks has never been so romantic. . . .

SRJUB-1